Meg Perry

Published to Death

A Jamie Brodie Mystery

Los Angeles, California

Monday, September 25, 2017

Chapter 1
Back to the Salt Mines

The Big Blue Bus rumbled up Wilshire Boulevard and hissed to a stop right in front of me. I stepped up from the sidewalk onto the bus with a deep sigh.

My sabbatical was over.

After eight weeks in the UK and four in New Mexico, I'd sent the second draft of the book I'd written - topic, Brodie family memoir in the context of Scottish history - to my editor at Oxford University Press last week. Today I was due back to my job as a librarian at UCLA's Young Research Library.

My husband, Pete Ferguson, and I had come home to Santa Monica on Saturday evening with scant time to regroup. We'd crammed laundry, restocking the pantry and a baseball game with my family into the past 24 hours. Pete was already four weeks into his latest career as an adjunct instructor in Arizona State's online psychology program, and his students' initial papers were coming due. I had three months' worth of email to plow through, and classes commenced on Thursday.

The coming week promised to be a whirlwind.

I went to work early to get the endless "how was your sabbatical?" questioning out of the way. I greeted everyone at the circulation desk, then my boss, Dr. Madeline Loomis. I said hello to the other librarians in the office suite and climbed the stairs to my second-floor digs, stopping in Liz Nguyen's doorway first. She wasn't alone. Avery Roth, until recently a librarian at Stone Canyon College and now a brand-new doctoral student in UCLA's history department, was in Liz's guest chair, her Doc Martens propped on the edge of Liz's desk. She grinned at me. "Hey! There's my personal librarian. Where have you been?"

I grinned back. "This is normal arrival time for me. Get used to it."

"Is your book published yet?"

"Lord, no. At least another six months. It's finished, though."

"Outstanding. I wish you were teaching my classes."

"Sorry, my adjuncting days are over. What are you taking?"

"200B and 204. Dr. Wolfe and Dr. Medeiros."

HIST 200B was Historiography, Ancient Rome, and HIST 204 was the required course for first-year students in how to be successful in the quest for a Ph.D. "You'll have a fantastic first quarter."

"I intend to. Do you have anything I can peruse as supplemental reading material to wow Dr. Wolfe?"

I gestured for her to follow me. "Come into my parlor."

Avery thumped her feet to the floor. "Later, Liz."

Liz fluttered her fingers. "See ya around."

Avery trailed after me into my office, where I retrieved a couple of books on Roman historiography from my shelves and handed them to her. "There you go. Some light reading before classes start."

"Thanks. What's your opinion of Caligula?"

I laughed. "That he was an unpleasant person. Why?"

"I might focus my research on him. Do you approve?"

"Sure. There's not much current research on him, so you'd have a niche."

"Cool. I'm off to the stacks. Later."

Avery disappeared down the hall and Liz entered my office. "Is the history department prepared for the whirlwind that is Avery?"

"She'll liven the place up, for sure. We should get to the meeting."

Our weekly librarians' meetings were held on Monday mornings at 9:00. Liz and I went downstairs to the conference room and joined the rest of the librarians. I sat beside Lola Mack, our classics librarian and said, "There's a new history doctoral student you should meet later on. She wants to write about Caligula."

Lola looked skeptical. "Is she aware of how few contemporary sources about him have survived?"

"I'm not sure. That's why she needs to meet you." I took a closer look at Lola; she seemed tired. "Everything okay?"

Her smile was intended to be encouraging, but it didn't convince me. "Yeah. Just didn't sleep much over the weekend. I'll get caught up."

Lola had a history of severe depression. She'd missed most of the fall quarter last year. I shook my finger at her in mock parenting style. "You'd better."

Her smile widened. "Yes, *sir*."

Dr. Loomis called the meeting to order just as our University Librarian, Dr. Laura Madorsky, entered the room. Dr. Madorsky didn't typically attend our meetings. Something must be up.

Dr. Loomis said, "First order of business is to welcome Jamie back into the fold. Your sabbatical was productive, I take it?"

"Yes, ma'am. The second draft of the book is finished and the editor has it now. It should be published in about six months."

Everyone applauded, and I responded with the royal wave, which produced laughter. Dr. Loomis smiled and said, "Wonderful. Our second order of business will be explained by Dr. Madorsky."

Dr. Madorsky pushed away from the wall where she'd been leaning. "You've probably seen flyers around campus announcing this... Beginning tomorrow and running through the end of the week, UCLA is hosting a convention of self-published authors on campus. The primary meetings will be at Carnesale Commons, but there will be sessions scattered throughout different buildings and the exhibit hall is in the Wooden Center. When you're out and about over the coming days and see a lost conventioneer, please guide them to their destination."

We all murmured agreement. Dr. Madorsky said, "Thank you. This is a convention of writers, so naturally it involves books. The self-publishing field is expanding rapidly, and it's an area in which academic libraries have had minimal impact. I'd like to change that. It's critical that we're aware of what's happening in all areas of publishing. Gina Marsh from Powell and Karen Lewis from the biomedical library are attending the conference, but I'd like to send one or two of you from YRL as well."

We all glanced at each other. Lola, the scholar of classical literature, looked horrified. Dr. Madorsky continued. "Much of self-publishing is in e-book format, and much of the marketing occurs through social media. Kristen, unless you have a compelling reason that you can't, I'd like you to attend. See what's trending in the world of book-related social media."

Kristen Beach - fellow librarian and my brother Kevin's girlfriend - was our communications and digital humanities specialist. Dr. Madorsky's request made sense. Kristen said, "I'd enjoy that. Thank you."

Dr. Madorsky smiled. "Thank *you*."

Kristen said, "I think Jamie should go, too. Since he's currently immersed in the publishing process."

What?? I said, "Uh…"

Dr. Madorsky raised an eyebrow. "Excellent idea. Jamie?"

Liz was smirking. Frank Villareal and Katrina Johnson were hiding smiles. I said weakly, "Sure. That'd be great."

"Wonderful." Dr. Madorsky handed Dr. Loomis a folder, which she passed down the table to us. "The conference schedule is in that packet. I'll look forward to your report. Madeline, thank you."

Dr. Loomis saw Dr. Madorsky out, then turned to us. "Kristen? Jamie? Do you have everything prepared for the new quarter?"

Unfortunately, I did. I'd combed through all of my research guides last week. I should have waited. I said, "Yes, ma'am."

Kristen said, "I do."

"All right." Dr. Loomis gave me an amused smile. "Looks like you're going to a convention. Now, third order of business…"

As soon as we were clear of the meeting room, I cornered Kristen. "You are a *rat*. You owe me, *big* time."

She grinned. "Oh, come on, it'll be fun. It's *different*. And we might learn something."

"You still owe me."

"I'll buy you a frappuccino right now."

"That's a start. You can buy my lunch today, too."

At noon, Liz, Kristen and I secured an outdoor table at the North Campus Student Center. A minute later, we were joined by Pete's sister and brother-in-law, Christine and Andy Fernandez, and their daughter - Pete's niece - Samantha. Sam was about to start her freshman year at UCLA and was moving into student housing this week. Once they were seated and had renewed acquaintance with Liz - they'd met at my wedding - I asked, "Sam, how's it going?"

"Super. I met my roommate. She's a Latina, too, from San Ysidro."

Chris said, "We moved everything in, but now we have to shop for stuff that we didn't realize Sam would need."

Liz said, "Oh, I remember doing that when I moved into the Stanford dorms."

Andy asked, "Are you from the Bay Area?"

"No, I'm from the Valley."

Chris said, "So you went away to school."

"I did." Liz smiled. "It was a wonderful experience. I'm sure it will be for Sam, too." Chris, Andy and the rest of the Fernandez clan lived near Tucson.

Kristen said, "Plus, Sam's surrounded by family here."

Andy said, "That does ease my anxiety. Sort of."

Sam shook her head at her parents. "I'll be *fine*."

Chris said, "Of course you will. But what kind of parents would we be if we didn't worry?"

At the reference desk, our regular patron and friend, former monk Clinton Kenneally, beamed when he saw me. "Dr. Brodie! Welcome home." He shook my hand vigorously. "I trust your sabbatical was fruitful?"

"Yes, sir. The book will be published in several months."

"Wonderful! I am eager to read it." He stepped back and assumed a more sober expression. "The word of the day is *divulgate*." He bowed and walked away.

Liz found the definition. "To make publicly known; to publish. That has double meaning for you, since you're headed to a publishing convention tomorrow."

"Don't remind me." I slumped in my seat. "I will *never* let Kristen off the hook for this."

Liz snickered. "Oh, come on. You'll have fun."

"Yeah? Wanna take my place?"

She grinned. "And deprive you of the experience? What kind of a friend would do that?"

Chapter 2
A Leopard Cannot Change His Spots

At dinner that evening, Pete was no more sympathetic to my plight than Liz had been. He laughed as I recounted what Kristen had done. "Oh, come on. You and Kristen will have a blast, gossiping about all the conference attendees."

I glared at him. "This had better not turn out like the conference in Oakland." Where we'd been derailed by a murder.

"Pfft. That's not possible. You're on your home turf."

"Hello? Most of the murders I've encountered have been on my home turf."

He dismissed that with a wave of his hand. "If the worst happens, you can duck out and retreat to your office. Are there any sessions on writing nonfiction? You might learn something."

I said grudgingly, "Maybe. I haven't read the program yet. But my book's already written."

"You might decide to write another one." He poked the back of my hand with his fork. "You're very grumpy pants about this."

"I just got back to work! It's -" I searched for a word. "Disruptive to my sense of order."

He grinned. "You and your sense of order. You have rugby practice tomorrow evening, right?"

"Right." My first since I'd dislocated my shoulder last spring.

"See? Something to anticipate." He wiggled his eyebrows. "For me, too."

Our sex life had suffered on sabbatical, thanks to staying in other people's houses and B&Bs with thin walls and tiny showers while in the UK, and hosting our friend Abby Glenn at the house in New Mexico while she built furnishings for us. Fortunately, watching rugby almost always got Pete in the mood.

I said, "Hmmmm. Maybe I'll take advantage of that."

He grinned widely. "You can try. *Try*, get it?"

I laughed. A try in rugby was the equivalent of a touchdown in American football. "You made a rugby joke! I think I love you."

"You *think?*"

I held my fork like a microphone and started to sing the chorus of the old David Cassidy song. "I think I love you…" Pete joined in, and we eventually dissolved into laughter.

Our meal concluded far more lightheartedly than it began. As I was clearing the table, Pete said, "Oh, by the way, I thought I should call Aaron. We haven't seen him and Paul since we left."

Aaron Quinn had been Pete's best friend at Santa Monica College; like Pete, he'd resigned at the end of spring term in the wake of a promotion scandal in their department. He was now managing a psychology research lab at USC. Paul Thayer, his husband, was an interior decorator who owned a home-staging business. Pete had been Aaron's best man at their wedding, six months before ours.

I said, "Sure. Want to invite them for dinner over the weekend?"

"We don't have anything else scheduled, do we?"

"Nope. We can grill if the weather cooperates."

I cleaned the kitchen while Pete called. "Hey, Aaron. Yeah, we got back Saturday evening. Jamie went back to work today. Eh - teaching online is okay, but it's too early to tell whether it'll be sufficiently fulfilling to make it permanent. But it pays the bills." He chuckled. "Yeah, I know. Everything still copacetic at USC? Good. That sounds interesting. Sure, sign me up. Oh, even better."

I raised an eyebrow at Pete - sign him up for what? He made a "don't worry" gesture and said to Aaron, "Listen, Jamie and I wanted to have you guys over for dinner this weekend, if you can make it. *What?*"

Pete paused, listening, dismay spreading across his face. I closed the dishwasher and sat down across the table from him. After a minute Pete asked, "How long? *Shit.* How the hell did he explain that?" Another pause. "And it never occurred to him to mention this? Yeah, I know." He sighed. "Well, then, why don't *you* come over? Saturday is great. Around mid-afternoon? We'll fire up the grill. See you then."

He disconnected and tossed his phone onto the table. "You are not going to *believe* this."

I'd been listening to the conversation with an increasing sense of dread and made an educated guess. "Paul's done something."

"He sure has. He's been getting some action on the side since June."

"*Damn.* I take it he and Aaron didn't have any sort of understanding."

"Nope. Needless to say, things are somewhat tense between them at the moment."

"When did Aaron find out?"

"Last week. Paul left his phone lying on the bathroom counter with a text from this guy on the screen."

"Sounds like he meant to get caught."

"Yep. Cowardly bastard."

I said, "You know… I never mentioned this, because A, I thought I might have been imagining it, and B, I didn't want to give you any reason to feel uncomfortable around Aaron and Paul. But I always had the impression that Paul might enjoy being more than friends."

Pete frowned. "Did he ever say anything?"

"Not a word. I can't even tell you *why* I had that impression. Maybe his facial expressions sometimes, or an innuendo that might have been perfectly innocent."

"But you picked up on *something.*"

"Yeah. Like I said, I thought I might have imagined it."

Pete shook his head, disgust on his face. He slowly spun his phone on the table with one finger. "Your instincts are pretty good."

"So Aaron's coming over Saturday by himself?"

"Yeah. He's moved into their guest bedroom for now."

"Are they communicating?"

"Only about housekeeping matters. They're not discussing the infidelity yet."

"Suppose they'll work it out?"

"I don't know." Pete spun his phone again. "Nearly a year after Aaron started dating Paul, he learned that Paul had been cheating on his then-boyfriend for the first couple of months that he and Aaron saw each other."

"Ack. Once a cheater, always a cheater?"

"Maybe. It'll be difficult to socialize with them now, knowing this."

"If Aaron is able to get past it eventually, we'll have to as well."

Pete frowned. "Yeah. Eventually."

"What is he signing you up for?"

"Oh." His face lightened. "Writing a paper. He and his buddy that he works for - Phil somebody - are testing physiological responses in the prefrontal cortex to violence in video games vs. violence in movies vs. violence on the news. Measuring the differences, if any."

"That does sound interesting. How will you be involved?"

"Pull the sources for and write the review of literature. Aaron said that Phil hates doing lit reviews and would gladly welcome a co-author affiliated with Arizona State."

"Cool. If that's the case, you might get more than one paper from that collaboration. I can help you with the research."

He grinned. "I was hoping you'd say that."

We each grabbed a beer and went to the sofa to watch *The Quantum Gene*, a sci-fi thriller about genetics researchers, actually based in real science, which was one of our favorites. The show preceding it had ten more minutes to run. I said, "How was work today?"

"Productive. I spent an hour and a half-ish on each class and was done in five hours. I ate lunch and spent the afternoon in the garden. I could get used to this." He elbowed me. "You could do the same."

"Yeah, but with both of us here, sharing the same office - sharing the same *desk* - would that work?"

"Hm. Maybe not. But I bet it would in the Alamogordo house. *If* you wanted to teach online."

"That's a big if. Now that you're four weeks in, how does it compare to face-to-face classes?"

He wrinkled his nose. "It doesn't. I miss the direct contact with the students. It's like I said before - this is serving as filler until I figure out what I *want* to do."

I held my bottle up for a toast. "Here's to doing what you *want* to do."

He clinked his bottle on mine. "I'll drink to that."

Chapter 3
A Legend in Her Own Mind

The next morning, I dropped my rugby clothes at my office and went downstairs to collect Kristen. We headed out to meet Gina and Karen at the Powell undergraduate library.

Gina Marsh was one of the librarians at the Powell Undergraduate Library, a relatively recent alumnus of UCLA's information studies program. She'd taught fifth grade in the LAUSD system for a couple of years, then decided that librarianship was far more attractive as a career choice.

Karen Lewis was a medical librarian. Her second masters was an MSN, and she'd worked as an ER nurse for ten years before going to library school. She also wrote self-published murder mysteries featuring an ER nurse as amateur sleuth. I'd read them all. They were gory and profane, but morbidly entertaining and hysterically funny.

Gina and Karen were waiting outside and fell into step with us as we turned toward Carnesale Commons, the primary venue for the convention. I asked, "To what or whom are we being subjected today?"

Karen said, "The keynote speaker is one of the superstars of self-publishing. Her name is Mercedes Moran. She's made several million dollars selling 99 cent romance novels."

Gina asked, "Through Amazon?"

"There, and all of the other e-book sites. She doesn't have anything in print, but she has a backlist of at least 80 novels. She publishes one per month."

I said, "*Wow*. Is she writing them herself?"

Karen shrugged. "She doesn't credit anyone else. I downloaded a couple, just out of curiosity. They're standard boilerplate bodice rippers. The names and locations change, but the stories don't vary much."

Gina wrinkled her nose. "And people buy enough of them to make her a millionaire several times over?"

Kristen said, "Never underestimate the romance reader. Those women binge read. If they find an author they like, they buy everything she's ever written."

I said, "How do you know that? *Please* tell me you're not a secret romance fan."

She laughed. "No. My boss at my first job was. She read paperbacks because e-books didn't exist then, but she went to used bookstores and library sales and bought them by the *bushel*. Her devotion was impressive. And she belonged to a romance readers' group there in Spokane. There were about thirty of them."

We entered the large meeting room and nabbed seats in the back row. Most of the other attendees were attempting to squeeze in as closely as they could to the front of the room, where there was an elevated podium with a central mic for the speaker and a couple of seats on either side. As soon as we were seated, the rest of our row was filled by a collection of middle-aged and elderly ladies. One of them, a grandmotherly type wearing a bright green sweater, had brought her knitting; another opened a tablet to the *New York Times* crossword.

I scanned the room as the conventioneers swarmed in. I was nearly the only male there; a handful of others were gathered near the back of the room, on the opposite side from us. I said, "Where are all the men who self-publish?"

Karen said, "Romance and erotica are among the top sellers in self-publishing, and they're mostly written by women. I'm sure there are men at the conference, but they may be avoiding the keynote."

At the front of the room, a woman in a sleeveless dress went to the center mic. "Good morning, everyone! I'm Carrie Reed, events coordinator at UCLA, and on behalf of the university I'm delighted to welcome all of you to our campus. In your packets you'll find maps of the campus and restaurant locations in Westwood. If you have any questions or concerns, please don't hesitate to see me or one of the conference staff. We're here to ensure that you have a wonderful visit."

Everyone applauded politely. Ms. Reed said, "Now allow me to introduce the president of the Association of Self-Publishing, Sabrina Larson."

Sabrina Larson was a height-challenged, apple-shaped woman in a jacket and long skirt that weren't particularly flattering, but her voice could have belonged to a Marine drill instructor. She pulled the mic down to her level and bellowed, "Hello, readers and writers!"

About half the room hollered back, "Hello!"

"Welcome to Los Angeles! I'm thrilled to be here on the campus of one of the world's top universities, and I know all of you are, too. Keep your eyes peeled for movie stars - I'm told that Sunset Boulevard and Beverly Hills are right over there!" She flung her arm out to the south, in the wrong direction.

The crowd roared its approval. Kristen snickered.

Ms. Larson continued. "On behalf of the Association of Self-Publishing, I want to thank UCLA and the lovely folks here at Carnesale Commons for their gracious hospitality. Isn't this a wonderful venue?"

Sustained applause. Ms. Larson basked for a moment, then held up her hand. "All right. You aren't here to listen to *me*. Without further ado, I'm thrilled to introduce one of the shining stars of our business, the woman who put self-publishing on the map, the author of over eighty self-published books, all of them best sellers - Mercedes Moran!"

About three-quarters of the room cheered and leaped to their feet in a standing ovation. I stood up, too, curious, and saw that the other 25% of the attendees - mostly in the back of the room, surrounding us, and including the other men I'd spotted - were stationary, arms crossed, glaring at the woman now taking the podium. A couple of people's expressions were downright malicious.

Strange.

I hadn't clearly defined to myself what I expected a romance writer to look like, but realized that I'd fallen prey to a stereotype. I'd imagined someone far more feminine. Mercedes Moran was built like an East German shot put champion, and her gravelly contralto voice suggested years of heavy smoking. She growled, "Good morning, fellow authors! I'd like to thank Sabrina and the Association of Self-Publishing for inviting me to give the keynote address today. It's such an honor."

Applause from the front of the room. The crossword puzzle worker, immediately to my right, muttered, "Such a *mistake*."

Mercedes continued. "The question I'm asked most frequently is, 'What is your writing process?' I decided to answer that once and for all this morning."

The woman in front of Kristen turned to the woman in front of me and asked, "Do we give a shit about her writing process?"

The woman in front of me snorted in disgust. Kristen looked at me with a raised eyebrow. I whispered, "Not universally beloved, is she?"

Mercedes said, "I approach every day just as I would any other typical working day. I have breakfast, get dressed, and go to my studio, which is in a separate building in the rear garden of my home. I'm at my computer by 8:00, and I work for eight full hours, taking breaks every two hours."

The woman beside me said, "Whoop-de-frakkin'-doo."

I had to bite my lip to refrain from laughing. Mercedes said, "When I'm starting a new book, I write an outline first."

The woman in front of Kristen said, "Like hell. She uses the same outline for every book."

I whispered to Kristen, "This is like Mystery Science Theater 3000."

She whispered back. "I know, right?"

Mercedes continued. "Then I build my characters - their appearance, their clothing, their speech patterns…"

She droned on about characters, plot and dialogue for a while. The women around us were yawning. I was getting bored, too. I began flipping through the program and list of exhibitors but glanced up at the sound of loud applause. "Is she done?"

Kristen said, "She's done with her writing process."

But Mercedes wasn't through. "Now I want to say a few words about the future of self-publishing."

The woman beside me said snarkily, "This oughta be good."

"We face a crisis in our profession - a crisis of authenticity. Too many authors hide behind pseudonyms. Too many authors hide behind *multiple* pseudonyms. This deceit is bad for business. You who are participating in this charade - your readers would be *appalled* to discover your true identities."

An undercurrent of unease was spreading through the room. I leaned across Kristen to ask Karen, "Is it common to use pseudonyms? I know you do."

"Yeah, it is." Karen was concerned. "She's potentially pissing off a lot of these people."

Mercedes growled, "How would the fans of Carmen Hidalgo feel to learn that their supposed Spanish princess was really a middle-aged housewife in Arkansas named Edna Brown?"

A gasp and murmur sounded from across the room. The woman in front of Kristen said, "Uh oh."

Mercedes wasn't done. "And yet that fraud is *nothing*, comparatively speaking. How many of you are fans of Angelica Ashley?"

Angelica Ashley? I whispered, "Holy *crap*." Angelica Ashley was the author of the best-selling erotic romance of all time - the Rose trilogy. *Rose, Rise; Rose, Rising; Rose, Risen.*

And I knew who Angelica Ashley really was.

About half the room applauded; another significant number had raised their hands. Mercedes wore a satisfied smirk. "Would you be surprised to learn that the Rose trilogy was written by a *man*? That behind Angelica Ashley was a man named *Elmer Thrash?*"

Gasps and various other sounds of shock ricocheted around the room. A male voice from the opposite side of the back aisle shouted, "So what? He's still a better writer than you!"

There were cries of dismay from the front of the room and loud applause from the back. I said to Kristen, "This is getting ugly."

She frowned. "Maybe we should…"

Then someone stood up in the middle of the aisle, and the room fell silent.

I whispered, "Oh, *no*. That's Martie Pepper."

Kristen said, "Who?"

There was a mic on a stand in the center of the room, intended for questions from the audience. Martie Pepper - first ex-wife and only heir of late TV host Dixon Gill, AKA Elmer Thrash - pulled the mic out of its clamp and turned it on. "My name is Martie Pepper. I was married to Elmer when he wrote the Rose trilogy. Accusations of deception are rich coming from *you*, Moran, when everyone in this room knows that *your* first five books were born as fan fiction of Rose. Talk about *deceit*. Your writing is derivative, plagiarized *dreck*. Why don't you tell them about the copyright infringement lawsuit I've filed against you?"

The room exploded into shouting and gesticulating. Gina leaned over and said, "I'm uncomfortable with this."

Karen said, "Me, too. Let's go."

I said, "The exhibits open in ten minutes. We can be the first ones there."

We scooted our chairs backwards so we wouldn't have to crawl over people, and ducked out the door. Even after it closed behind us, we could still hear angry voices. Mercedes and Martie were still at the mics, and a dozen other people were trying to shout them both down.

Karen said, "Well. That was - unusual."

Kristen asked me, "Who's Martie Pepper?"

I explained about Elmer Thrash/Dixon Gill and the Rose trilogy. "I know who she is because she was involved in the case of that actor who was killed last year. The one Abby discovered in his pool."

Kristen said, "I remember. You were researching a problem with the script."

"Yeah. Pete and I met Martie on set the day Jon wrapped the case."

Gina's eyes were wide. "Wow. I harbored the notion that romance writers were nice people."

Karen said, "Not all of them, obviously. Listen, there's a breakout session on mystery writing next, being held on the second floor. I want to go to that."

Gina said quickly, "Oooh, mysteries. I'll come."

Kristen said, "Jamie and I will check out the exhibits. See you later."

Kristen and I left the building and crossed to the walkway that would lead us past the track and field stadium and the intramural fields to the Wooden Center. When we entered the exhibit hall, we saw that it was divided into sections - one area for companies offering print publishing services to e-book authors, one area for cover artists and independent editors, one for indie publishing companies and one for authors.

We found the men that had been absent from the keynote speech at author tables. Male writers of sci-fi, spy thrillers, and military nonfiction crowded one aisle. Kristen said, "I suppose they didn't think there was anything to learn from Mercedes Moran."

"I suspect they were right." I looked around, and a sign caught my eye. *M/M Romance*. I nudged Kristen. "Look at that."

"Male-male romance? Have you read any of that?"

"No. I wasn't aware that it existed."

We approached the table, which was sponsored by a small publisher that apparently specialized in the genre. The woman at the table smiled up at us. "Hello! Are you male-male romance fans?"

I said, "I've read a lot of gay mystery, but I didn't realize that gay romance was a thing."

"Oh, yes! We publish many best-selling authors in this genre." She tipped her head and gave me an amused look. "As long as you're not averse to reading gay sex scenes."

I laughed. "Nope. Not averse to that at all, as long as they're realistic."

The woman grinned. "What brings you to the conference?"

Kristen said, "We're UCLA librarians. Our boss sent us on a scouting expedition."

"Wonderful! Do you carry much fiction in your library?"

I said, "No, but we're from the graduate research library. The undergraduate library has a more extensive fiction collection."

"Of course." The woman handed us each a card with the name and website of the publisher. "If you have a chance, check out our website and authors. And remember, writers earn more if you buy directly from the publisher."

Kristen said, "We'll remember."

We wandered away as I studied the card. Kristen said, "You might enjoy that."

"Gay romance? Yeah, and it might be the gay version of Mercedes Moran." I wrinkled my nose. "Did you see the authors' names on the books at her table? Mostly women."

"So?"

"So, women writing about sex and romance between men? That feels - odd."

"Maybe their gay friends have told them about it."

I gave her a sideways look. "Don't get any ideas."

She grinned and poked me in the arm. "You're awfully cynical about a genre you've never read."

"I'm not sure it appeals to me. And the covers - those headless torsos? All of them sporting six-packs? Bizarre."

"You should go to the website and read the blurbs. Maybe there are some that are mystery-romance combos."

Chapter 4
Armed to the Teeth

In the next aisle, we found ourselves in the mystery section. There were quite a few men here, although women were well represented. I said, "I wonder why Karen didn't get a booth here?"

Kristen shrugged. "It may have been too expensive. I bet each of these tables cost several hundred dollars."

"Whoa. There go her profits for the year."

"Precisely."

We wandered down the aisle, nodding and smiling to people, but not stopping - until we were brought up short by a display of *weapons*. A middle-aged man was seated behind a table; several books, firearms prominently displayed on their covers, were stacked in front of him. Behind him was a pegboard on which hung a variety of guns and knives, a tire iron and an ice pick. An eye-catching display if ever there was one. I pointed at the board and asked the guy, "One for each book?"

"Oh, no." The guy gestured at the board. "Those are actual murder weapons. I was a cop for twenty years. This collection consists of the weapon used in each case we investigated over that time."

No police department on the planet would allow homicide evidence to be released to an ex-cop for display *anywhere*. Not to mention that he'd *never* be granted permission to bring them onto this campus. I edged closer to the pegboard and scrutinized the guns.

Actual murder weapons, my ass. I'd been raised by a Marine gunnery sergeant and knew my firearms. The guns hanging from the board were replicas. The knives, tire iron and ice pick were real, but could have come from anywhere.

I performed a silent count of the items. There were twelve. A murder every two years? He hadn't worked for any police department in Los Angeles County. I said, "Where were you a cop?"

He drew himself up proudly. "Tequesta, Florida."

Never heard of it.

Kristen said, "You must have plenty of material for writing mysteries, then."

"Oh, sure." He lifted an eyebrow. "You wouldn't *believe* some of the things we see in South Florida."

I didn't doubt that. "Has anyone ever used an alligator to commit a murder?"

He laughed. "Now you're veering into Carl Hiaasen territory there. In real life, the perps aren't that inventive."

Kevin, a homicide detective himself, had said once that cops never uttered the word *perp*. I wondered if this guy had been the Barney Fife of South Florida.

Kristen said, "You have the most unique display here, that's for sure."

"Thanks." He nodded at our name badges. "You're UCLA employees?"

I said, "Yes, sir."

"Do you folks enjoy a good mystery?"

Kristen said, "We do."

He handed us each a book. "There you go. The first in my series, on the house. I hope you'll like it well enough to buy the rest. And tell all your friends."

"Thank you!" Kristen and I said it together.

"No problem. Have a good day, now."

As we walked away, I examined the cover more closely. The background was composed of a pile of money and a stack of what I supposed were kilos of cocaine. A gun, with a wisp of smoke exiting the barrel, was in the foreground. The author's name was Guy Testaverde.

Kristen took out her phone. "Let's see. Tequesta, Florida - ah. Population 5,629."

"Plenty of material for writing mysteries, huh?"

She grinned. "I can't *wait* to read this."

Chapter 5
We Could Sell Tickets

We turned a corner and found ourselves in the M/F romance section. The entire aisle was populated by writers and publishers of romance. Kristen said, "*Wow*."

We strolled down the center of the aisle, looking at the poster-sized covers that ranged from chaste to lurid. I said, "Everything from Bibles to bondage."

"I wonder if your Martie Pepper has a table here?"

"She's not *my* Martie Pepper, and the Rose trilogy was published by one of the big houses. How do you suppose a self-published book ever makes it to the bestseller list?"

Kristen said, "It almost never does. But Amazon has its own bestseller lists for every sub-sub-genre. A reader can find the best sellers in whatever miniscule category they're searching for." She stopped suddenly and picked up a book from a table. "Check *this* out."

The title of the book was *The Laird and the Lawyer*. The cover depicted a chiseled man in a kilt, naked to the waist, embracing a woman wearing a business suit. Kristen asked, "Whose plaid is that?"

"Royal Stewart." The most ubiquitous of setts, AKA tartan patterns. I'd recognize it anywhere.

The woman behind the table had been speaking to someone else; now, she turned to us with a smile. "Hello! Are you romance fans?"

I said, "Sorry, no."

Kristen said, "He's an author. An expert on Scottish history."

I wouldn't go *that* far - but I didn't correct Kristen because I figured I knew what she was up to. The woman's wide smile dimmed slightly. "Oh. How interesting."

I said, "Yes, ma'am, it is. Does your plot feature the Stewarts?"

That puzzled her. "No... Why?"

"Your cover model is wearing a Royal Stewart kilt."

She snatched up one of her books, scowling at the cover as if the model had deliberately chosen the wrong plaid. "He *is?* Does that matter?"

Oh. My. God. Kristen smirked at me. I said, "Er, well, it depends on your level of concern with regard to historical accuracy."

The author goggled at me. "Oh. Um. I *do* research - but none of my readers have ever complained."

I asked, "What clan is your laird?"

"Campbell."

Oh, jeez. The Stewarts and Campbells were mortal enemies, back in the day. My expression must have telegraphed how stricken I felt. The author frowned. "It's a minor detail, right?"

Kristen, the rat, was attempting not to laugh. I said, "Sure. Minor. Unless a Campbell or Stewart reads the book. No one else is likely to care."

"Well. I guess I'll have to take my chances." The woman glared at me. "Thanks for your help."

I suspected that she didn't mean it. I said, "Sure," and dragged Kristen away from the booth.

As soon as we were out of earshot I said, "Expert? Seriously?"

"You're far more of an expert than *she* is. From the expression on your face, I assume that the Stewarts and Campbells weren't besties?"

"You assume correctly." I glanced at the booths we were passing; kilts were featured prominently on many of the covers. Most of them were Royal Stewart. I sighed inwardly. "Has Kevin modeled his kilt for you yet?"

While in Edinburgh, I'd ordered kilts for myself, Pete, and Kevin. My dad and my brother Jeff already owned Brodie kilts. I'd sent Kevin his kilt when we'd arrived in New Mexico.

Kristen snickered. "Oh, yes. It's quite flattering."

I held up my hand. "*Please* don't include details."

"Hey, you asked. If Kev and I got married, would I be eligible to wear a Brodie kilt?"

"Yeah. Although women traditionally didn't wear kilts. *Are* you two discussing marriage?"

She was nothing if not nonchalant. "Oh, well, it's come up in conversation a couple of times."

I gave her a skeptical look. "Uh huh."

She just grinned.

We'd reached the center of the aisle when people started flowing around the far corner from the opposite direction. I stopped. "Looks like the keynote let out. I don't see any blood."

As soon as I said *blood*, there was an explosion of raised voices at the far end of the aisle. People who had already arrived turned to see what was happening. Kristen said, "You may have spoken too soon."

I said, "Let's go around. We'll never get through that way."

We hurried back along the preceding aisle and approached the disturbance from the opposite direction. Mercedes Moran was standing in the center of a knot of women, her arms folded. She was being confronted by a short woman who was being restrained by a couple of other ladies. The angry woman was yelling. "How *dare* you! What business is it of yours?"

Mercedes said, in a snootily superior tone that made *me* want to punch her, "The fans have a right to know."

"You think so, huh? Are you sure that you don't have anything in *your* past that fans have a right to know? I just might look into that."

Kristen leaned over to a woman standing at the edge of the circle. "Who is the shorter woman?"

"Ruth Zwick. She writes as Bethany May. Mercedes outed Ruth on Facebook and Twitter last Friday."

I said, "Outed her?"

"Divulged her true name and identity. It's Mercedes's mission, or something. She's done it to lots of romance writers."

Kristen said, "Do the readers care?"

The woman shrugged. "I don't. Good writing is good writing. But some readers feel betrayed if an author turns out to be someone other than the person they'd imagined. It can impact sales, and it always causes turmoil on social media."

Kristen was about to ask something else when Ruth broke free from the women restraining her and charged Mercedes like an angry bull, head-butting her right in the solar plexus. Mercedes made an "oof" sound but didn't fall. She grabbed Ruth's hair and pulled. Ruth screeched and scratched.

A couple of youngish men drifted over from a sci-fi display. One of them perked up. "Cool! Catfight!"

No one was attempting to stop the scuffle. Most of the women had their phones out, recording it. I scanned the crowd and realized that I was the tallest and fittest person there by far. I waded into the fray and dragged Ruth away from Mercedes, lifting her off her feet and depositing her back into the care of her friends. "*Enough.*"

Mercedes straightened the scarf around her neck. "Who the hell are you?"

I said, "I'm the guy who's gonna call the cops if you two don't shut it."

She drew herself up. "Do you know who I am?"

"I don't give a shit if you're Mercedes Moran or Queen Elizabeth. I work here at UCLA, and I *will* cause trouble for you if you don't make yourself scarce right now."

A few women applauded. Mercedes stared daggers into me. I said, "Oooh, scary. Now get out."

"Fine." Mercedes pointed at Ruth Zwick. "But I'm not done with you, bitch."

Ruth lunged at Mercedes again, but her friends held on this time. The fracas had attracted the attention of a couple of UCLA cops who must have been assigned to the exhibit area. One of them - Officer Armstrong, according to his nametag - asked, "Everything okay here?"

I showed him my BruinCard and said, "It will be, if one of you will escort Ms. Moran out of the exhibit area."

"Yes, sir. Ma'am, if you'll come this way…"

Mercedes flounced out ahead of the two officers. I said to the remaining crowd, "The rest of you behave."

One of them purred, "Anything you say, gorgeous."

Kristen started to laugh. I said, "*Stop* it. Let's get out of here."

It was nearly noon. Kristen and I had promised to meet Samantha for lunch, since her parents were going to be at our house visiting with Pete. When we got to the table, Sam was already there with another girl who had terrible acne and the glossiest hair I'd seen outside of a shampoo ad. Sam said, "This is my Uncle Jamie and my sort-of aunt, Kristen." She indicated her friend. "This is my roommate, Ysabel Candelaria."

We shook hands with Ysabel, who said, "I'm glad to meet you."

Sam said, "We've been at the LGBTQ center. They have a group for Latinas."

I said, "That's smart. The sooner you get connected on campus, the sooner you feel at home."

Ysabel said proudly, "I identify as asexual. I'm so happy that the LGBTQ center recognizes us as part of the community."

I smiled. "Good for you." I was secretly glad that Sam's roommate was something other than straight, although I was surprised by her boldness.

"My family believes it's not a real thing." Ysabel sighed. "I keep trying to educate them."

Kristen said, "That's all you can do."

Sam asked, "How's the convention?"

Kristen said, "Jamie had to break up a fight between two romance authors."

Ysabel wrinkled her nose. "Ugh. Romance." She put the back of her hand to her forehead, fluttered her fingers, and said in falsetto, "Oh, Chahhhhles, what*evah* shall we do? Father has promised me to Lord Fauntleroy."

We all laughed. I said, "Ysabel, you might have a future on the stage."

She grinned. "Nah. I'm a marine biology major. But thanks."

Chapter 6
Dead as a Doornail

After lunch, the girls headed for the bookstore and Kristen and I returned to the convention center. The afternoon sessions included several on social media, so Kristen disappeared in the direction of those rooms. I read the program and found nothing of interest. The sessions relating to nonfiction were scheduled for tomorrow.

I decided to visit the exhibit hall one more time then go back to my office. If I could work for a couple of hours each day, I wouldn't fall behind. I wandered through the exhibits, collecting pens, sticky notes, fridge magnets, and other goodies for Liz and myself. I found myself passing the M/M Romance table again, which was now being manned by a man. I stopped and said, "Hi."

He stood and shook my hand. "Hi. I'm Nate Gardner. Are you a male-male romance fan?"

"Until this morning I didn't even know it existed. I read a lot of gay mystery. Can I ask you something?"

"Sure."

"What's with the headless torsos?"

He chuckled. "Yeah, some readers find those disturbing. The thought is that if readers don't see a face on the cover, they're free to imagine for themselves what the characters look like."

"Huh."

I must have looked skeptical; Nate laughed. "What gay mystery authors do you read?"

"Neil Plakcy, Anthony Bidulka, Richard Stevenson, Dorien Grey…others, too. Can I ask you something else?"

"Of course."

"Why are so many of the writers female?"

He spread his hands and shrugged. "Romance writers as a whole are overwhelmingly female, regardless of subgenre. And most readers of male-male romance are women. There are lots of theories as to why."

I pointed to a couple of books. "The ones who use initials, are they women too?"

"For the most part. Do you object?"

"No... It just seems odd to me to have women writing about what goes on in gay guys' bedrooms."

"That's understandable. But give it a try. Our authors are among the most popular in the genre."

"I will."

Nate handed me a card. "If you order this week and use the code at the bottom of the card, you'll get free expedited shipping."

"Thanks, I'll do that."

I pocketed the card and turned away from the booth, intending to go back to my office. I'd just entered the main aisle when a tall, sturdily built, middle-aged woman I didn't recognize scurried past me, then spotted me and turned, gasping for breath. "You! You work here, right?"

"Yes, ma'am... why?"

She grabbed me by the arm and began to tug. "Something terrible has happened! You have to do something!" She began dragging me toward the back of the room.

"Uh - ma'am? Should we call the police?"

She didn't answer but hauled me behind the heavy gold curtain made of velvet-like material that formed the rear wall of the display space. "There!" She pointed.

A body was lying about 50 feet away. I couldn't see her face clearly, but her size, hair color and clothing, not to mention the blood pool she was lying in, indicated that something terminally unpleasant had happened to Mercedes Moran.

Bloody hell. I couldn't help myself. "Jesus fucking Christ on a *cracker*. Not *again!*" I turned to the woman who'd brought me and asked, "Why were you..."

She was gone.

Shit. I stuck my head outside the curtain and saw the woman's back rapidly disappearing into the crowd. I made as many mental notes as I could - dyed red hair, brown sweater, long skirt - then retrieved my phone from my pocket and called 911.

I didn't recognize the two UCLA cops who arrived while I was still speaking to the dispatcher. According to their name plates, they were Officers Cavanaugh and LoPietro. They scanned the scene with narrowed eyes. Cavanaugh asked, "Have you touched the victim?"

"No, sir. I haven't stepped beyond this point."

LoPietro pulled a phone out of his uniform pocket and began snapping photos, documenting the floor ahead of his footsteps as he approached the body. When he reached Mercedes he squatted and felt for a pulse. He straightened, took several more pictures without shifting position, then retraced the same path he'd traversed to the body. "She's dead. Still warm. I'll call Pope."

Cavanaugh turned to me. "Who are you?"

I showed him my BruinCard and told him where I worked. He snapped a photo of my ID - both BruinCard and driver's license - and asked, "Why did you come behind the curtain?"

"A woman dragged me down here. She'd found the body and was kinda hysterical."

Cavanaugh was attempting to maintain a neutral expression, but skepticism was written all over his face. I didn't blame him; I wasn't sure I'd believe me either. "Where is this woman now?"

"She left before I called you guys." I described her.

"Why'd she pick you?"

"I don't know. She might have recognized me." I told him about the fight between Mercedes and Ruth Zwick. "Officer Armstrong and his partner walked Mercedes out after they talked to me."

"Uh huh." Cavanaugh turned to LoPietro, who'd ended his call to whomever Pope was. "Call Armstrong, willya? Ask him about a fight this morning."

LoPietro called. Cavanaugh's gaze fell back on me. "Where did you go after the fight?"

"I left the building with my co-worker, Kristen Beach. We bought lunch at Panda Express and met my niece and her roommate at the North Campus Student Center. Then I came back here. I walked around gathering loot -" I showed him the bag of swag I'd accumulated - "then stopped to talk to the guy at the Loving Men Publishing booth. I'd just left him when the woman who found the body ran up to me."

"What can you tell me about Ms. Moran?"

"Very little. I'd never heard of her until this morning." I told him how I came to be at the convention and about the ruckus at the keynote speech.

Cavanaugh raised an eyebrow. "So the lady didn't have many friends?"

"It seemed like she had plenty of friends, but also plenty of enemies."

"What were the names of the two women she mentioned in her speech?"

"The first one was Edna something from Arkansas. Edna Brown, maybe? The other was a local woman, a TV executive named Martie Pepper."

Cavanaugh's level of suspicion was nearly through the roof. "And *you* know this because…"

I sighed. "Because I aided LAPD on an investigation involving her, about a year and a half ago."

He nodded slowly, disbelief bleeding from every pore. I could read his thoughts. *You're awfully tangled up in this.*

I pinched the bridge of my nose.

LoPietro was now stringing crime scene tape around the scene. Cavanaugh was about to say something else when more UCLA cops appeared on the scene.

One of them, fortunately, was Antonio Jenkins, whom I'd come to know over the past few years. He was surprised to see me. "Dr. Brodie? What are you doing here?"

"My boss made me come to the convention. I broke up a fight between the victim and another woman a few hours ago."

A guy with sergeant stripes who seemed to be a supervisor - the aforementioned Pope - said, "Do you know the other woman's name?"

"Ruth Zwick." Too unique to forget.

"She's attending the conference?"

"Yes, sir."

"And who did you say brought you back here?"

I described the woman to the best of my ability. Pope turned to his men. "LAPD is on the way. Brown, Jefferson, you start canvassing the exhibitors. Cavanaugh, LoPietro, you've got this guy's story?" *This guy* being me.

Cavanaugh said, "Yes, sir."

"Good. See if you can track down the Zwick woman. All of you, keep an eye out for this mystery lady. Jenkins, Kerrigan, you two guard the scene."

The uniforms scattered. Pope said to me, "You, stay. LAPD will want to talk to you."

"Yes, sir." I didn't doubt that for a second.

Pope began taking more photos with his own phone. I waited at the edge of the curtain with Antonio, who asked, "This is a book convention?"

"Yeah. Dr. Madorsky thought the libraries should be represented. She made Kristen and me both come."

Antonio grinned. "Not your thing, eh?"

"*No.*"

A few curious people approached; Antonio shooed them away. I hadn't paid attention before but now noted that the exhibit hall was extremely noisy. If there had been an argument behind the curtain before Mercedes was killed, I doubted that anyone would have heard it.

Chapter 7
Calling In the Cavalry

About ten minutes later, Kevin and his partner, Jon Eckhoff, ambled into view. Kevin shot a look at me but didn't say anything. He and Jon introduced themselves to Pope, who provided the details, leaning heavily on my involvement. "We've called the coroner and photographed the entire scene. Give me your email address and I'll send you the photos."

"Thanks." Kevin spelled out his address.

Pope tapped his phone, sending the pictures. "There you go. What else can we do for you?"

"If you could round up these women - what were their names?"

Pope consulted his notes. "Edna Brown, Ruth Zwick, and Martie Pepper."

Jon said, "Martie *Pepper?*" He looked over at me. "*Our* Martie Pepper?"

Apparently Martie Pepper was mine, whether I liked it or not. "Yeah."

Jon started laughing. Kevin just shook his head. "Anyway, Sergeant Pope, if you could locate those ladies and hold them at your station, we'd appreciate it."

"We're on it. I'll call you when we have them." Pope gestured to me. "What about him?"

Jon smirked. Kevin said, "Don't worry. We'll handle him."

"All right." Pope looked back and forth between Kevin and me, frowning. "You two related somehow?"

I kept my mouth shut. Kevin said, "Yes, we are. I guarantee his complete cooperation."

Pope wasn't entirely satisfied with that, but said, "Okay. He's your problem, then."

Kevin said, "You have no idea. Thanks for your help, Sergeant."

Jon provided his phone number to Pope, who left. Kevin rested his hands on his hips and scanned the area. I said, "I'm your *problem*, huh?"

Kevin grinned. "Would you *rather* be Pope's problem?"

"No, *thank* you. They believe I found the body and that the mystery woman who dragged me back here is total fiction. I'm their primary suspect."

Kevin crossed his arms. "You didn't kill her, right?"

"*What??* Of *course* not, you nimrod! I'm gonna…"

He punched me in the shoulder. "Come on. I'm just winding you up."

I glared at him. "Well, cut it the fuck *out*. I'm having an *incredibly* shitty day, in case you hadn't noticed. Where's that social worker compassion?"

Kevin was studying for an MSW through the online program at Simmons College. "I'm not licensed yet. Can't practice without a license."

I shot him double birds; he just grinned. Jon said, "What a week for Tim to be sick."

Tim Garcia was Kevin's former partner, now the supervisor of the detectives' unit at West LA Division. I said, "What's wrong with Tim?"

Kevin said, "Emergency appendectomy over the weekend. We'll call Jill and Elias if we need help." Jill Branigan and Elias Pinter, the other two homicide detectives at West LA.

Jon said, "Or the lieutenant. Get some honest work out of him."

Kevin snickered. "Yeah, right. With campus cops canvassing, we'll be okay."

Jon asked, "What's Martie Pepper doing here?"

"She's suing the victim for copyright infringement." I recounted the confrontation at the keynote speech. "The victim's books were originally fanfiction of the Rose trilogy that Elmer Thrash - Dixon Gill - wrote."

Jon snorted. "Damn, that guy just won't stay *dead*. What's fanfiction?"

"Where fans of a book - or a TV show or movie - write new stories using the same characters from the book or show. There's tons of it online."

Kevin looked mystified. "Why would they do that?"

"If they're creative types, they may be immersed in the world built by the original author and enjoy writing new stories for it. And some of it's X-rated. There's a whole community of people who write Star Trek stuff where Kirk and Spock are doing each other."

Jon laughed. Kevin said, "That's *sacrilege*."

I grinned. "That's fanfiction."

"So why would Martie sue if this is a common thing?"

"It's okay as long as it stays unpublished. But Mercedes Moran apparently made millions of dollars using characters that were based on Dixon's. Elmer's. That's illegal."

A squad of LAPD forensics technicians appeared, led by a skinny young guy. "Detective Brodie?"

Kevin turned. "Hey, Adam. According to UCLA PD, there hasn't been much traffic back here. See what you can turn up."

"Yes, sir." Adam and his minions began unpacking equipment.

Jon glanced back along the aisle. "There are hundreds of people here."

I said, "And hundreds more in the sessions at Carnesale. That's where Kristen is."

Kevin and Jon both turned their backs to the exhibit area and watched the forensics techs work. One was vacuuming, one was snapping more photos, one was dusting every available surface for fingerprints, and one was searching along the base of the curtain. None of them were approaching the body yet. Jon asked, "When did you see her alive?"

"Late morning. Probably 11:45 or so. I know it was almost noon because as soon as the cops escorted her out, Kristen and I left to have lunch with Sam and her roommate."

Jon checked his watch. "It's 2:45. How long have you been back here?"

"Twenty minutes, maybe?"

Kevin said, "So she's only been dead an hour or two. If she…"

A voice from behind Kevin and Jon said, "You boys must be Detectives Brodie and Eckhoff."

Chapter 8
Bad News Travels Fast

Kevin and Jon turned, moving apart as they did. A man had appeared behind them and was now looking back and forth between them, his chubby face beaming.

The guy looked like the love child of Yogi Berra and Santa Claus. He was in his early sixties, about 5'7", round-bellied and rosy-cheeked, with thinning gray hair in a fringe around the back of his head. He was wearing a camel sport coat, brown plaid pants, and a badge hooked over his chest pocket.

The man stuck his hand out to Kevin. "Lieutenant Nelson Hopkins. I'm taking the reins for Detective Garcia on this case while he's on medical leave."

Kevin shook his hand. "Yes, sir. Ah - we weren't told to expect you."

"No worries." Hopkins shook Jon's hand. "I'm not here to steal your thunder. I'm a team player all the way. But, as you can imagine, the chief and the mayor take a dim view of prominent visitors to our fair city going home bagged and tagged. The powers that be decided to keep their collective fingers on the pulse of this investigation, to forestall a firestorm of bad publicity." He beamed again. "You know how it is. You can't fight city hall."

Jon and Kevin exchanged a glance. Hopkins held up his hands, palms out. "I know, I know. I wasn't born yesterday. I can tell, you two are about as happy to see me as an outbreak of the plague. But let's not get off on the wrong foot. I'm not here to rain on your parade. We're all in this together."

I was already envisioning a drinking game, where we'd take a shot for each of Hopkins's clichés but realized we'd be blind drunk in under fifteen minutes. A slow smile was spreading across Jon's face - he was enjoying this. Kevin was trying to maintain a neutral expression, but I could tell he was thinking, *What the hell??*

Hopkins held his hand out to me. "And you are?"

I shook his hand. "Dr. Jamie Brodie, from UCLA. I was attending the conference."

Hopkins eyed me. "Brodie, eh? I'll take a wild guess and say that you and the good detective here are related."

I said, "Yes, sir."

Jon said, "Jamie's helped the police in several investigations. He's also a librarian. This is a publishing conference, so we thought we'd take advantage of his expertise on this case."

Oh, great. I glared at Jon; he returned a smirk. Hopkins gave me an appraising look, then clapped his hands together twice. "*Excellent* idea. You'll give us a leg up. Help us level the playing field and hit the ground running."

Hoo boy. "Yes, sir."

Hopkins grinned. "Far be it from me to look a gift horse in the mouth. Welcome to the party, Dr. Brodie."

I smiled wanly. Hopkins clapped both Kevin and Jon on the shoulder. "I've heard great things about you two, batting near a thousand with that solve rate. Head and shoulders above the rest. You're making the movers and shakers downtown sit up and take notice, I can tell you that. I'm just happy to be here, to ride on your coattails for a while."

Jon said, tilting his head toward Kevin, "That's mostly him."

"No, no, let's give credit where credit is due. Don't hide that light of yours under a bushel. I know your partner agrees with me one hundred percent, right?"

Kevin said, "Right. One hundred percent."

Hopkins said to Jon, "I've been around the block and back, son, and I know a good team when I see one. You cease and desist on that modesty stuff. It's not needed."

I said, "There's no I in team."

Kevin's scowl deepened. Jon's grin widened. Hopkins nodded happily. "Exactamundo! Takes one to know one, or so they say. I bet you're a pretty sharp cookie yourself, am I right?"

Jon said, "He's nothing to sneeze at."

Kevin bit his lip to keep from groaning. Hopkins clapped his hands together again. "Okay, boys. I could stand here talking 'til I'm blue in the face, but we should get this show on the road. Apply our noses to the grindstone and put the finger on our bad guy. Or gal, as the case may be."

Jon said, "I'm as ready as I'll ever be. Let's roll."

I followed Jon, Kevin, and Hopkins a few feet into the space behind the curtain, to the perimeter that the UCLA police had established around Mercedes Moran's corpse. They donned paper booties and crossed under the yellow tape. I sidled over to where Antonio Jenkins was manning the border. "LAPD headquarters sent a lieutenant down here to assist in the investigation."

Antonio nodded at Hopkins. "That guy?"

"Yeah. Nelson Hopkins."

"He from Homicide Special?"

"He didn't say." Although that would make sense. Homicide Special was usually called out on celebrity murders. Not that Mercedes Moran was a major celebrity.

Kevin, Jon and Hopkins were circling the body, looking it over. I called to them, "This morning during the fight, I noticed that Mercedes was wearing a neck scarf."

Jon scanned the area behind the curtain. "Not here now. She might have left it in her room, though."

True. Kevin knelt by Mercedes's head and studied the body, his head tilted. "Is the ME here yet?"

Antonio raised his voice so Kevin could hear. "On her way."

Hopkins said, "A penny for your thoughts, Detective Brodie?"

"Looks like a puncture wound to her neck. The angle of entry might give us a clue as to the height of the killer."

Jon squatted on the other side of Mercedes. "Huh. Awful lot of blood for such a tiny wound."

Hopkins looked confused. "I don't get your drift, Detective Eckhoff."

Jon straightened and scanned the area around Mercedes. "Arterial spray, with a void…" He pointed. "There. The killer stood there and would have gotten blood all over himself. Or herself."

Kevin said, "Lucky shot, hitting the carotid with the first blow? Or someone with a knowledge of basic anatomy?"

Hopkins let out a low whistle. "Well, knock me down with a feather. You boys *are* the real deal." He scrutinized Mercedes's body and the splatter pattern. "Your expertise is a joy to behold, and I don't mean maybe. *Amazing*. I am..." He threw up his hands. "I am at a loss for words."

I doubted that. Kevin's face expressed his bemusement at Hopkins's overreaction. Jon said, "Aw, Lieutenant, this is just the low-hanging fruit."

Kevin groaned audibly. From the far end of the row of curtains, the assistant ME and her crew appeared. The AME stepped under the yellow tape and stopped beside Kevin. "Who do we have here?"

Kevin said, "Mercedes Moran, romance author."

"Not anymore." The AME snapped on gloves and knelt beside Mercedes's body, studied it for a minute, then waved one of the forensics techs over. The tech used several lengths of sticky tape to collect potential evidence from Mercedes's jacket. The AME reached into the jacket's pockets. "Empty. Did she have a purse?"

Jon said, "Not with her."

Kevin asked, "Angle of entry?"

The AME squinted at the neck wound, then asked a tech for a magnifying glass and studied it more closely. "Hard to say. My initial impression is that it's angled downwards, but I'll have to dissect it out to be sure."

Jon said, "Anyone who stabbed Mercedes from above would have to be pretty damn tall."

Hopkins lowered his voice. "We'd better keep a lid on this information. Don't want the public to get wind of this. If anyone lets the cat out of the bag, it could muddy the waters of our investigation."

Jon said, "Yes, sir. Our lips are sealed."

Kevin pinched the bridge of his nose. The AME stood up, looking skeptically back and forth between Jon and Hopkins. "Oooookay. Kevin, I'll call you when we're ready to transport."

"Thanks, Doc." Kevin led Jon and Hopkins out of the taped-off area to where Antonio and I were standing.

Hopkins said, "All right, boys, let's put our thinking caps on. What's the 411 on our victim?"

I explained what I knew about Mercedes Moran. Hopkins nodded in the direction of the exhibits. "All of these folks are writers?"

"Or people who are trying to sell services to writers."

"Packed in here like sardines, aren't they?" Hopkins turned back to Kevin and Jon. "I can't help but notice... a lot of these ladies, you'd have to call 'em pleasingly plump, wouldn't you?" He shook his head sadly. "And so many of them have pretty faces."

Kevin winced, and Hopkins saw his reaction. "I know, I know. In this day and age, that's not politically correct. I've been through the diversity training. Sometimes, though, I've just gotta call 'em as I see 'em."

I said, "Now, Lieutenant Hopkins, if you can't say anything nice…"

He held up his hands in surrender. "I hear you. You hit the nail on the head." He sighed. "Old habits die hard. Anyway. You think this might be a case of the ol' green-eyed monster at work?"

Kevin said, "Yes, sir."

Jon said, "It's a fine kettle of fish, for sure."

Hopkins slapped Jon on the shoulder. "I like the way you think, Detective. You and me, we're on the same wavelength."

Kevin sent me a beseeching look. I returned a tiny shrug.

Hopkins scanned the room again. "What's the game plan, fellas? I'm thinking we need to divide and conquer, vis à vis questioning this cast of thousands."

Kevin said, "All available UCLA PD officers are canvassing. They're going to detain anyone they think we should interview and bring in the three women that were identified as having words with the victim earlier in the day. They're also pulling security camera footage for us."

"Sounds like a plan." Hopkins grinned. "I gotta tell ya, it's great to be back here in my old stomping grounds."

Jon asked, "West LA?"

"Right. Of course, that was when you two were still just twinkles in your daddies' eyes. But back in a former life, when I was young and foolish, I was a patrol officer here in West LA for a few years." He smiled reminiscently. "Those were the days. But then windows of opportunity began to open, and I ended up downtown."

I asked, "Are you Homicide Special?"

He looked at me in surprise. "No, no. Did I not tell you from whence I came?"

Kevin said, "No, sir."

"Well, that was an oversight on my part. But it's no secret. I'm an open book. I ride a desk in IAG."

Internal Affairs Group. Kevin and Jon looked at each other, not entirely hiding their dismay. Hopkins noticed. "Now, boys, keep your pants on. My boss likes to send us out in the field every so often to get a breath of fresh air, so to speak. See which way the wind is blowing on the streets. When a supervisor is on leave, like your Detective Garcia, he sends one of us when he can to plug the hole. This is just meant as a learning experience for me. Now." He clapped his hands together again - obviously his signal for *saddle up*. "Where are we going to set up shop?"

Jon's phone rang. He answered, "Eckhoff. Wonderful. Thanks, Sergeant. We'll be right there." He hung up and said, "UCLA PD has corralled our three persons of interest. They've offered us the use of their shop."

Hopkins said, "Excellent. Let's make hay while the sun shines, boys."

Chapter 9
A Case of Mistaken Identity

We left the Wooden Center and headed across campus. We were about halfway to our destination when Jon said, "We're being followed."

Hopkins said, "What?"

We turned and found ourselves face to face with three startled women, probably in their late twenties, conference badges dangling from their necks. They were wearing matching t-shirts, bearing a movie logo that I recognized all too well...the logo of the *Fast and Furious* franchise.

Kevin said, "I believe this one's for you, short stuff."

The girls were all staring at me in disbelief. The one on the right said, "It *can't* be."

I smiled sadly. "You're right, it can't."

The girl in the center said, "But you look *exactly*..."

I held up my hand. "Thank you. It's an enormous compliment. But I don't look *exactly*." I stepped toward them and leaned in. "See? Hazel eyes. Not blue."

The girl on the left said, "Those could be contacts."

"Now why would I do that?" I held out my BruinCard for inspection. "My name is Jamie Brodie. I've worked at UCLA since 2006." I pointed to the date printed on the card.

Miss Conspiracy Theorist on the left said, "ID cards can be faked."

"Seriously? Again, *why* would anyone do that?"

Miss Conspiracy Theorist frowned. "I don't know. But it's possible."

I tried to be gentle. "I'm sorry. It's *not* possible. You must realize that."

The girl in the center decided to test me. "When were you born?"

"May 17, 1980."

"*Where* were you born?"

"Camp Pendleton."

"What's your sister's name?"

"I don't *have* a sister." I beckoned to Kevin. "If you don't believe me, ask him."

Kevin produced his badge and stepped forward. He'd had to intervene on this topic before. "I'm Detective Kevin Brodie, Los Angeles Police Department. I'm Jamie's brother, and we have no sisters." He stuck his face next to mine. "See how we look alike?"

The girl on the right was becoming convinced. "Yeah, you do. Heather, it's not him."

Miss Conspiracy Theorist - was she Heather? - said, "That badge could be faked too."

Oh, for God's sake. Behind me Hopkins said, "You might just have to agree to disagree with these ladies, Dr. Brodie."

Kevin sighed and lifted the corner of his jacket, displaying the holstered gun on his hip. "Does that look fake?"

The girl in the center gasped and took a step back. "*Whoa.*"

Miss Conspiracy Theorist said, "I don't know…"

I retrieved my phone and flipped through my wedding photos until I found the one I wanted. "That's not faked either. The guy on the right is my *husband.*"

Miss Conspiracy Theorist squinted at the screen. "Oh. *Oh.*" She stepped back, dismayed. "Well, crap."

Jon said, "A picture is worth a thousand words, huh?"

Kevin grimaced. "We have work to do, guys."

The girl on the right said, "Sure. Sorry to bother you." She grabbed the girl in the center firmly by the arm and tugged. "Come on, Desiree."

The ladies departed, Desiree and Heather giving me one last backward glance. As we walked away Hopkins asked, "What put the bee in those girls' bonnets?"

I told Hopkins who I'd been mistaken for. He said, "Hm. Guess I'm behind the times. The name doesn't ring any bells."

I said, "I keep hoping people will move on."

Jon said, "Don't hold your breath."

Behind me Kevin muttered, "Shut up and walk."

Chapter 10
The (Un)Usual Suspects

When we reached the UCLA PD station, Sergeant Pope met us at the door and escorted us to a conference room in which I'd been before, when UCLA PD was investigating the theft of a score from the music library. Kevin said, "Is there a one-way mirror in here?"

"There is."

"Could you put Jamie behind it, please?"

Pope was astonished. He must have expected that I'd be the interrogatee. "You *sure* about that?"

Kevin shot him a narrow look. "Yes."

"Oooookie dokie." Pope's tone said, *It's your funeral*. He opened the next door down, which led into a narrow, cramped room that appeared to be primarily used for storage. "Sorry about the dust." He didn't sound sorry.

"Thanks." I took a puff from my asthma inhaler and settled in to watch the proceedings.

When I'd been in the conference room previously, the one-way mirror had been covered by a screen. Now the screen was up and I could see the entire conference room. Ruth Zwick was pacing the room; she turned as the door opened. "*Finally*. What's this about?"

Kevin said, "I'm Detective Brodie and this is Detective Eckhoff and Detective Hopkins from LAPD. We'd like to ask you a few questions. Please have a seat."

"*LA* PD??" Ruth sat. She seemed genuinely puzzled as to why LAPD might want to question her. "What's going on?"

Jon said smoothly, "No reason for concern, ma'am. Can you tell us about your relationship with Mercedes Moran?"

Ruth's face grew red. "Is *that* what this is about? The fight I had with that bitch this morning?"

Kevin said, "Tell us about that fight."

"*Well*." Ruth smoothed her skirt with her hands. "To answer your first question, we don't *have* a relationship. I'd never met her until this morning." She sighed. "I write romance novels. I publish under a pen name because Bethany May is a far more romantic name than Ruth Zwick. My friends and family all know, but my readers didn't - until Mercedes announced it on her blog last Friday."

Jon asked, "How would she have found out?"

"I have no idea, but I'm not her only victim." Ruth scowled. "She specializes in outing authors. Exposing their true identities."

I noted two things: that Ruth was referring to Mercedes in present tense and that Hopkins wasn't saying a word. He was taking notes but keeping his promise of not interfering so far. Jon said, "Would your readers care what your real name was?"

"The ones with any sense know that we use pen names. The others…" Ruth picked at her nail polish. "I posted about it on my own blog, and the comments section blew up. Most of my readers defended me, but a few felt 'betrayed.'" She used air quotes. "It got nasty for a couple of days, then I closed the comments."

Kevin said, "Will it affect your sales?"

"It's way too soon to tell." Ruth shrugged. "It's not like I make that much money anyway. I taught school for thirty years. The income from the books pays for my health insurance until I turn 65. It's not the money, it's the *principle*." She started getting mad again. "Mercedes has no right to do what she does, and there's no reason for it. None of us are a threat to her financially. She's just a nasty bitch."

The thought crossed my mind that Martie Pepper and her lawsuit might pose a financial threat to Mercedes. Jon said, "Ms. Zwick, you were overheard threatening to expose something about Ms. Moran. Is there anything to expose?"

Ruth sagged. "Not that I'm aware of. Other writers have searched for dirt and failed. Mercedes Moran is her real name, we know that. No one else can uncover anything. She's the best at keeping her personal life hidden."

Kevin said, "All right, Ms. Zwick. After you confronted Ms. Moran, where did you go?"

"Back to my hotel room. Mercedes had yanked my hair out of whack and I wanted to fix it."

"Did anyone go with you?"

"Yes, two of my writer friends. Then we went to lunch." Ruth gave Kevin a curious look. "Why?"

Kevin wasn't ready to tell her. "What are your friends' names?"

"Alice Carver and Rhonda Schumann."

"Where did you go to lunch?"

"We left campus and went to a pizza place nearby. I believe it was called 800 Degrees. *Why?*"

"How long were you there?"

"A couple of hours. We had just returned to the room when the police came. WHY?"

Jon said, "Mercedes Moran was found dead in the exhibit hall at around 2:15 this afternoon."

Ruth's state of stunned shock looked genuine to me. She stared for a minute, then said, "*No.*"

Jon said, "I'm afraid so."

"And you think… No. I would *never*. Yes, Mercedes is a bitch, but who would *kill* her?"

Kevin said, "Let me ask you that question. Who would kill her? Has she outed anyone that was truly harmed by being exposed?"

"Not that I know of. I mean - I don't know the circumstances of everyone she's outed, but the result for the author is typically no worse than embarrassment. I've never heard anything that was worth *killing* for."

Jon and Kevin shared a look, and Jon said, "Ms. Zwick, we appreciate your cooperation. If you have the phone numbers for your friends that you had lunch with, we'll call them right now and get this cleared up for you."

Ruth recited the numbers. Jon said, "Thanks. I'll be right back." He left the room.

I stepped out of the observation room and met him in the hallway as he was calling. He crossed his eyes at me as he said, "Hello, Ms. Carver? This is Detective Jonathan Eckhoff, Los Angeles Police Department. No, no. Everything's fine. We're just following up on the altercation between Mercedes Moran and Ruth Zwick earlier today. Can you tell me what happened there?"

He listened for a minute. "Okay. What did you do then? Where? How long were you there?" He gave me a thumbs-up; Ruth's 800 Degrees story must have held up. "What did you do then? All right, that's just fine. No, Ms. Zwick isn't in any trouble. Thank you for the information." He hung up. "So far, so good."

I said, "It doesn't sound like she knows that Mercedes is dead yet."

"No." He called the second number. "Ms. Schumann?"

Jon's end of the conversation was nearly identical to the one he had with Ruth's first friend. When he hung up I said, "Corroboration?"

"Yep. Except that Ms. Schumann added that a handsome young man had pulled Ruth off of Mercedes."

I smiled coyly. "I do what I can."

He grinned. "What you can do now is get back in the obs room. We'll let Ruth go and bring in the next contestant."

I said, "I can't wait to see your reunion with Martie Pepper."

"Uh huh. We're saving her for last."

I resumed my observation post. Jon gave Ruth the good news that her friends had backed her up. She said, "Because that's what *happened*. Can I go now?"

Kevin said, "Yes. Thank you again for your cooperation. If we could ask one more thing of you?"

Ruth gave him a narrow look. "What?"

"Don't spread the word that Ms. Moran was killed. We'd like to keep it as quiet as possible for now."

Jon said, "I didn't mention it to your friends. They think we were investigating your fight with her."

Ruth said, "I'll try."

Kevin said, "That's all we can ask. Thank you."

Jon escorted Ruth out of the room and returned with another middle-aged white woman, who established her identity as Edna Brown, from Little Rock.

Hopkins was still sitting quietly, a benign smile on his face, taking notes. I was amazed that he hadn't chimed in yet.

Maybe he really was trying to learn something. I wondered how long it had been since he was actively involved in an investigation.

Kevin said, "You write romance novels, correct?"

"Yes, in my spare time. My daughters and I own a florist shop."

"Do you use your own name?"

She laughed. "Goodness, no. Who would read a romance written by Edna Brown? I use the name Carmen Hidalgo."

Kevin asked, "How many people know your real name?"

Edna made a sound of annoyance. "A lot of them do now, I guess. I understand that Mercedes Moran announced it in her keynote speech this morning."

"You weren't at the keynote speech?"

"No. I went with a couple of friends to the La Brea Tar Pits."

"Did you know that Ms. Moran intended to expose you?"

"No, but I'm not surprised she did. She's made that her latest hobby." Edna shrugged. "It's not a big deal to me. I say in my bio, in the books, and on social media that Carmen is a pen name. I don't announce what my real name is, but I don't panic if people find out."

"Do you think it will impact your sales?"

"I doubt it." Edna laughed. "I have a unique readership. My books are sci-fi lesbian romance and my heroines are all lesbian science nerds. That sort of thing doesn't appeal to the average romance fan. I'm a sub-subgenre of one, as far as I know. My readers will keep reading."

I made a note of the name Carmen Hidalgo. Sci-fi lesbian romance sounded like something Sam might enjoy. Kevin asked, "Have you met Ms. Moran?"

"No."

"When did you get back from the tar pits?"

"We didn't come straight back. We had lunch at the art museum and walked around the grounds there. We'd just returned to our room when the cops showed up." Edna tipped her head. "What the heck is going on?"

Kevin asked, "Do you happen to have receipts from this morning?"

"I do." Edna dug into her purse and handed over two receipts. Jon snapped photos of them and handed them back.

Kevin said, "Thank you. Do you know many other romance writers?"

"No. My friends that I came with are readers, not writers. I don't participate in a lot of the online romance sites because my subject matter is so - er - out there."

"Do you know of anyone that would have any reason to harm Ms. Moran?"

Edna looked alarmed. "Not at all. Has something happened to her?"

Jon spoke for the first time. "Ms. Moran was found dead in the exhibit hall at about 2:15 this afternoon."

Edna's jaw dropped. As with Ruth, I seriously doubted that she'd known of Mercedes's demise. "You are *shitting* me."

Kevin's lip twitched into a fleeting smile. Jon said, "I'm afraid not."

Edna shook her head in astonishment. "I can't *imagine*." She gathered herself a bit. "I can promise you it wasn't me."

Kevin said, "No, ma'am, your receipts show that you were elsewhere at the time of the murder. We'd appreciate it if you'd refrain from speaking about this to anyone."

"My friends know I was brought here."

Jon said, "That's okay. Ms. Moran was involved in a fight earlier in the day. You can tell them that's what we're investigating and we interviewed you because your name came up in the keynote."

"Okay." Edna blinked. "*Wow*."

Jon handed Edna a card. Kevin said, "If you remember or overhear anything that might be helpful to us, please call."

"I will."

Jon saw Edna out, then stuck his head through the door of my room. "Need a break?"

"Yeah." I stepped into the hall and lowered my voice. "Why isn't Hopkins saying anything?"

"I don't know, but I'm glad he's not."

"Maybe he is really here to learn."

Jon looked skeptical. "A lieutenant from IAG, brushing up on his homicide investigation skills? I doubt it."

"Then why is he here?"

"Beats me. If we can get rid of him later, maybe we can call around and find out. Right now, I've got to take a leak before we start with Martie."

I bought a Coke from the station soda machine and concealed myself behind the mirror again. Jon went into the interview room, and Kevin left. A minute later he returned with Martie Pepper.

Chapter 11
Déjà Vu All Over Again

Martie was taken aback to see Jon. "Detective *Eckhoff?* What's going on?"

Jon said, "It's a pleasure to see you again, Ms. Pepper. You've met my partner, Detective Brodie, and this is Detective Hopkins. How's The Gravity Channel going?"

Martie owned The Gravity Channel, which aired *The Quantum Gene*. The original script for the pilot was one of those that I'd investigated in the Rafe Conroy murder a year and a half ago. "Gross income has doubled since we began, thank you. You're a *homicide* detective. What the *hell* is this about?"

Kevin said, "Mercedes Moran was found dead in the exhibit hall about an hour ago. Murdered."

I knew Martie had done some acting, but I didn't think she could fake the reaction she had. She gaped, her chin nearly to her collarbones. "*What??*"

Kevin said, "If you would, tell us about this lawsuit you've filed against Ms. Moran."

Martie huffed out a breath. "Oh, for God's sake. You can't possibly suspect…" She caught Kevin's expression - *You're not answering the question, and that makes me suspicious* - and said, "I'm suing her for copyright infringement. The plots and characters of her first five books are clearly plagiarized from the first Rose novel."

Jon asked, "You still own the rights?"

"Yes. Dixon had sold the film rights, but I recently bought them back. The print rights were never sold."

Kevin asked, "How was the suit progressing?"

"It wasn't. Her lawyer kept filing ridiculous motions." Martie crossed her arms and glared at Jon. "In order to win my case, I needed Mercedes *alive*. Why would I jeopardize that?"

Kevin said mildly, "Might be easier to win if you're suing the estate, not the woman."

Martie shook her head vigorously. "No. I want to see her *lose*. I want to push her to the brink of financial *ruin*. I need - needed - her *alive* for that." She made an exasperated noise. "*Dammit.* Whoever killed her has stolen that from me. I was *so* looking forward to that."

I believed her. Jon said, "Tell us about the keynote speech."

Martie related the details of the keynote just as I'd observed them. "When I said I was suing Mercedes, the place went crazy. People were shouting back and forth and there was some shoving. Mercedes was bleating on about something, but I took the opportunity to educate her deluded fans about the similarities between her books and Dixon's."

Kevin asked, "How long did that go on?"

"Only about five minutes. Two women appeared and hustled Mercedes offstage. I decided I'd made my point and got out of there."

"Where did you go?"

"To my attorney's office. I had an appointment with him anyway about another matter, and I told him what I'd done." Martie sighed. "That took about an hour and a half, including the drive. Then he and I went to lunch at Knead, which took another hour. Then I drove home, where I found the police waiting."

Jon took contact information for Martie's lawyer. Kevin asked, "Can you think of anyone who would want Mercedes dead?"

Martie shook her head. "I know very little about the romance publishing field. Dixon - Elmer - wrote the books while we were married, but he was already married to his second wife by the time the trilogy was published. I didn't realize that Mercedes's books were knockoffs until a friend told me about it." She sniffed. "I don't read romance. I prefer science fiction. When I learned who Mercedes was, I read her entire blog. I'd been on the fence about suing - I thought I might contact her and come to an agreement - but when I read her posts and learned what a bitch she was, I decided to nail her to the wall."

Jon said, "Ms. Pepper, we appreciate your cooperation. If you think of anything else that might be useful, please call."

"I will." Martie stood and pocketed Jon's business card. "Believe me, I want to know who did this. I might just sue them, too."

Jon saw Martie out and returned to the hallway as I met Kevin and Hopkins there. Sergeant Pope stuck his head out of his office, frowning. "Based on our canvassing so far, no one admits to seeing the victim at *all* after she was escorted out of the exhibit hall this morning. And no one noticed *anyone* go behind that curtain at *any* time."

Jon said, "The exhibit hall was swarming and incredibly noisy. Mercedes and her killer might have gone unnoticed."

Kevin asked, "Any sign of our mystery woman yet?"

"No." Pope scowled at me. I attempted to look innocent.

Jon and Kevin thanked Pope for his help and we left the police station. Hopkins, who hadn't spoken since the interviews began, blew out a breath. "Well, I don't know about you boys, but I could stand to wet my whistle. Is there any place on campus to get a cup of Joe?"

I said, "There's a coffee shop in our library."

"Perfect!" Hopkins beamed. "Lead on, MacDuff."

We entered YRL and found seats in Café 451. Hopkins looked around in approval. "Nice place you've got here."

I said, "Thank you."

Hopkins sipped his coffee appreciatively. "Mm. That hits the spot." He smiled at us genially. "Are you boys married?"

It seemed odd that he didn't want to discuss the case. Kevin looked as if he thought the same. He said, "They are. I'm not."

I asked, to be polite, "Are you?"

"You bet." Hopkins leaned back and hooked his thumbs in his belt. "Thirty-eight years next month."

Jon said, "Congratulations."

Hopkins reached into his jacket and pulled out his wallet. He produced a picture of himself standing behind a sweet-looking lady about his same age. "Four sisters, and not a bad one in the bunch, but my Ellen was the pick of the litter."

I said, "She looks like a nice lady."

"Ab-so-tively." Hopkins smiled at the picture. "I'll let you in on a secret - she's got me wrapped around her little finger. I let her rule the roost. I'm man enough, I don't need to wear the pants in the family."

Kevin said, "It's not easy being married to a cop."

"You hit the nail on the head." Hopkins tucked the wallet back in his jacket. "But I've never been married to the job. Ellen wouldn't stand for that. It might have cost me a few rungs on the ladder, but what's more important, I ask you?"

Jon said, "Family, first and foremost."

Hopkins pointed at Jon, but addressed Kevin and me. "You heard it here first."

Jon's phone rang and he checked the ID. "Ah. Martie's lawyer." He answered, "Detective Eckhoff. Yes, sir. Can you tell me when you met with Ms. Pepper today?" He listened for a minute and gave us a thumbs up. "Yes, sir. I appreciate that." He spelled out his email address. "Thank you." He hung up. "He's emailing me the restaurant receipt."

Hopkins said, "We're barking up the wrong tree, boys. Ms. Pepper's got an airtight alibi. It's back to square one." He grinned widely. "I've gotta tell you, I'm loving this. I've been riding a desk downtown since Hector was a pup. It's *great* to be back in the saddle again."

Once again, I wondered what the hell Hopkins was doing here. He drained his coffee and clapped his hands together - his signal for impending action. "Let's get out of Dodge, whaddya say? Go someplace where we can grab some grub and chew the fat about this case. I'm as hungry as a horse."

I checked my watch and stood. "I hate to drink and run, but I have to call it a day. I need to get to rugby practice."

Jon snickered. Kevin pressed his fingers against his temples. Hopkins looked up in surprise. "Rugby, eh? Good for you. All work and no play makes Jamie a dull boy, you know what I'm saying?"

"You said it." I slugged Kevin playfully in the shoulder. "Later."

Chapter 12
The Plot Thickens

Pete, accompanied by our yellow Lab, Ammo, picked me up twenty minutes later. On the way to Griffith Park, I related the details of the day.

Pete was as mystified as I was about Hopkins's purpose. "No way did IAG send him out to get field experience. Something else is going on."

"Kevin thinks so too, but he can't ask around until they get rid of Hopkins. Which might not happen for a while."

Rugby practice was low-key. About a third of the players had been practicing over the summer, about a third of us hadn't, and about a third of the participants were new to the team. We warmed up, ran drills with and without the ball, took care of some team business and adjourned.

When I got to the sidelines, Pete was nearly drooling. "*Damn*, I've missed this. We're heading straight home, right?"

I laughed. "Yes, and you're driving so I can see your hands at all times."

At the car, I checked my phone and saw that I had a text from Kevin. *Call when you're done at rugby.*

I called as Pete drove us home. "Hey, what's up?"

"Turns out that until eight years ago, Mercedes Moran was a programmer in Silicon Valley named Tammy Thomas. The startup she worked for was struggling and offered buyouts to select employees. Tammy accepted the offer. Six months after that she moved from San Jose to San Francisco, legally changed her name, and started writing fan fiction. Six months after *that* she published her first novel."

"Huh. Ruth Zwick said that people have tried to find dirt in Mercedes's past. Why wouldn't they have been able to uncover her name change?"

Kevin said, "They didn't dig deeply enough into court records, I guess. Anyway, when you have a chance tomorrow, see if you can find anything in your databases on Tammy Thomas."

"Will do. Is Hopkins still with you?"

"No, thank God. He said he's a creature of habit and had to get home to his blushing bride."

I laughed. "Hey, a man's home is his castle."

Kevin groaned. "Don't you start. I just got Jon to stop."

In the background I heard, "Got me to stop what?"

I said, "Are you at the station?"

"Yeah. We were doing follow-up interviews with people on campus until just about an hour ago. And we still have to search Mercedes's hotel room tonight."

"Anything from the security cameras?"

"No." I could hear the disgust in Kevin's voice. "The area behind the curtain isn't covered. Can you believe that?"

"I bet that'll change. Have you had a chance to find out what Hopkins is up to?"

"No. I was going to ask the captain, but she'd gone home by the time we got here. I'll catch her in the morning."

Jon had moved closer to Kevin's phone. "We're going above and beyond the call of duty!"

Kevin groaned. I said, "Yeah, but it's a labor of love, right? Just be careful you don't burn the candle at both ends, or you'll look like death warmed over in the morning."

"Gack! I am hanging up *right now*. I'll talk to you tomorrow."

I said, "Nighty night, sleep tight…"

He hung up on me.

I laughed. Pete glanced over, smiling. "What?"

"Jon and I are playing along with Hopkins in the cliché-spouting game, and we're driving Kevin crazy."

He grinned. "Driving him bananas? To drink? Up the wall? Around the bend? Off his rocker? Off the rails?"

I snickered. "Ex*act*ly. You're good at this."

"Uh huh. So your dead author has a secret past?"

"Not much of one. She legally changed her name when she became a writer. That's all."

Pete drummed his fingers on the steering wheel as he drove, thinking. "A puncture wound to the neck, right?"

"Yeah, possibly from above - and Mercedes was at least six feet tall. How does that even happen?"

He considered that. "Ice pick, I guess. Although - who brings an ice pick to a publishing conference?"

I froze. "Oh, my *God*. An ex-cop mystery writer, that's who." I dialed Kevin's number again.

Pete said, *"What??"*

Kevin answered tiredly. *"What?"*

"Could that puncture wound have been caused by an ice pick?"

"Sure, if the killer was tall enough. Why?"

"Because Kristen and I saw one today." I told him about our encounter with Guy Testaverde. "He didn't stand up, so I don't know how tall he was."

"Oh, for God's sake. Now we've got to track this small-town cheeseball and see if he still has his ice pick with him?"

"Hey, you're the detective. I'm just giving you some food for thought. Consider it a goodwill gesture."

He hung up on me again.

Pete glanced at me. "Do you think this Testaverde guy could have crossed paths with Moran?"

"I don't know. They wrote in different genres, but… You should have been in that conference hall. She's made a *lot* of enemies."

When we got home, Pete's enjoyment in watching rugby practice spilled over into his libido, as I'd hoped. After a vigorous session on the bedroom floor - always a hoot with Ammo sniffing around us - we took a shower then collapsed into bed. Pete asked, "So are you going to check out this male-male romance stuff?"

"Sure. Some of it might be good."

He smirked. "Maybe it'll give us some ideas."

I laughed - but that was a thought. Pete had never been interested in watching porn with me, as it reminded him too much of the sexual abuse he'd suffered as a teenager at the hands of his parish priest. Maybe reading about romantic sex in black and white wouldn't be as traumatic.

Before we turned out the lights, I went to the Loving Men website, found two highly rated romances, and ordered them. With the shipping code, they'd arrive by Friday. Just in time for the weekend.

Chapter 13
Vanished Without a Trace

On the bus the next morning, I got a text from Kevin. *Meet us at Café 451?*

OK. Did you ask the captain about Hopkins?

Yeah. She doesn't know.

Is she going to find out?

She didn't think we should ask too many questions yet.

Don't rock the boat, huh? :-)

Stop it. See you shortly.

I put away my phone with a feeling of mild trepidation. Kevin had been previously investigated by IAG - technically, by the Force Investigation Division of IAG - for two officer-involved shootings, one in 2003 when he wounded a drug dealer while he was on patrol with Pete and one when he killed Hunter Mitchell in the lounge of the Hotel Bel Air four years ago. He'd been completely cleared in both instances - but could Hopkins's presence have something to do with that?

It seemed far-fetched. IAG wasn't known for their subtlety. If they were investigating Kevin, he'd surely know.

So what was going on?

When I entered the library building, I waved to Connie Bright at circulation and went straight to the coffee shop. Jon had already commandeered a table, and Kevin was at the counter paying for two coffees. He turned around just as the barista said, "Hi, Dr. Brodie! A mocha frappuccino?"

"You bet."

Kevin wrinkled his nose. "What the hell is that?"

"It's delicious is what it is. It's sort of a coffee milkshake."

He shook his head and went to the table. I paid and was taking my drink from the barista when I heard a familiar voice say, "Good morning! Another day, another dollar, eh? I'm bright-eyed and bushy-tailed. You boys ready to rock and roll?"

The look of despair on Kevin's face was priceless. Jon grinned. "Yes, sir. Ready, willing and *able*."

I joined them. "Morning, Lieutenant."

Hopkins seemed delighted to see me. "Wonderful! The gang's all here!" He sat down and put his hands on his knees. "So. What are our known knowns?"

I sat beside Hopkins, leaned back so he couldn't see my face and crossed my eyes at Kevin, who ignored me and filled Hopkins in on Guy Testaverde's background. "We tracked him down in the hotel bar last night."

Jon said, "He was three sheets to the wind."

Kevin sighed. "He sobered up fast, though, when we followed him back to his room and he couldn't find his ice pick."

Hopkins said, "Oho. A rude awakening, I bet."

I asked, "What was his explanation?"

Kevin said, "The moron stepped away from the display a couple of times to visit the men's room. He claims to have no connection whatsoever with Mercedes Moran, although he said he'd heard of her. So that's squirrelly. And he can't prove that he was at his booth when Moran was killed."

Jon said, "The tire iron was missing, too. He's deep in the dog house with the LAPD."

I said, "Too bad you can't arrest him for being dumber than a fence post."

Kevin rubbed his eyes. "We learned last night that Mercedes Moran's name was originally Tammy Thomas. No marriages, no kids, no family that we can locate. The company she programmed for went bankrupt a couple of years after she left them. We're trying to locate former employees."

Hopkins said, "Who was in the know about Thomas becoming Moran?"

"No one, so far. But when we searched her room, we found her phone. Jill is going through it, identifying her contacts."

Hopkins stroked his chin. "Hm. I'm thinking that one of these online attacks came back to haunt her."

Kevin said, "Yes, sir. There's no evidence so far that it's related to her programming career."

I said, "That dog won't hunt."

Kevin closed his eyes. Hopkins lightly smacked the table in front of me. "You've got a good head on your shoulders, young man."

I elbowed him playfully. "Takes one to know one. Sir."

He laughed and slapped his knees. "What do you say, fellas? Time to saddle up?"

Jon and Kevin were both looking over my shoulder. Jon said, "Not just yet."

I twisted in my seat, only to see Kristen approach. "Lieutenant Hopkins? I'm Kristen Beach. Detective Brodie's better half."

Kevin gave Kristen a look of utter dismay. Hopkins scrambled to his feet - as did the rest of us - and shook Kristen's hand. "It's a pleasure, Ms. Beach. Detective, I thought you told me you weren't married."

"No, sir. We're not married yet."

Yet? I raised my eyebrows at Kristen, who smirked. Hopkins said, "Well, then, what are you waiting for? When are you gonna tie the knot, son? Make an honest woman of her?"

Kristen came to Kevin's rescue. "Ah, Lieutenant, don't give Kevin a hard time. It's not him, it's me."

I snickered. Kevin asked, "What are you *doing* here?"

"It occurred to me just a few minutes ago. Yesterday when Jamie and I saw Mercedes Moran and Ruth Zwick fighting, another bystander told us that Mercedes specialized in outing other authors through social media. Revealing their true identities. She'd just done it to Ruth Zwick last week."

Hopkins looked confused. "Sure - the blog thing, right?"

"Yes, but it's likely that Mercedes had far more than a blog. Most successful self-publishers market themselves *extensively* on social media. Facebook, Twitter, blog tours, Instagram, Goodreads, all the rest. If Mercedes made her enemies on social media, you'd have to read through *all* of her sites to identify potential suspects. That would take you forever, and you wouldn't even be able to access some of the sites without an account. I know none of these three have Facebook or Twitter accounts, for instance. But I do, and I can search through all of that." She grinned. "See if your victim had any other skeletons in her closet."

Hopkins was delighted. "That is a stroke of genius. I never cease to be amazed by the wonders of modern technology. Ms. Beach, I leave it in your capable hands. Full speed ahead with that plan."

"Yes, sir." Kristen held up her fist for a bump from Kevin. "See ya later, alligator."

Kevin bumped her fist with a sigh. Jon said, "Keep us in the loop."

"You betcha." Kristen grinned at me and walked away.

Hopkins watched her go, admiration written across his face. "That young lady's a force to be reckoned with. I bet you've got your hands full with that ball of fire."

I said, "She's in a class by herself."

Kevin glared at me. Jon said, "She'll dig up a gold mine of information for us. She might be able to blow this thing wide open."

I murmured to Kevin, "Not married *yet?*"

He whispered back, "It's come up in conversation. Although if she keeps spouting clichés with the rest of you, I'm gonna have second thoughts."

Chapter 14
A Concerned Citizen

We drained our coffee and split up, agreeing to regroup in a half hour. Hopkins said he had a couple of phone calls to make; he went outside. Kevin and Jon went to confer with Kristen about her social media hunt, and I went to my office to check email.

Fifteen minutes later, I was in the middle of an email, making an appointment with a student for next week, when Kevin and Jon appeared. Kevin flopped into one of my visitor chairs. "We think we might know why Hopkins is here."

"Why?"

"Because of you."

My hands froze on the keyboard. "*What?*"

Jon said, "It's just a theory, but the possibility exists. Our captain knows that we occasionally outsource research to you, and she's okay with it, but... what if the word has made it up the line?"

I was stricken. "Is that a problem?"

Jon spread his hands. "The captain has signed off every time. We have it in writing. We assume her supervisor knows, but maybe it never went any further. Until now."

"Then why hasn't Hopkins said anything to me?"

Kevin said, "He may only be observing and reporting back. You've seen that legal pad he's filling with notes. Maybe the notes are about our interactions with you."

"Well, shit. What should I do?"

Kevin stood up. "For now, nothing. We may be wrong. Just act normally."

I glared at him. "How am I supposed to do that *now?*"

That only earned me a shrug. From both of them.

We met Hopkins outside and headed back to the Wooden Center. Kevin and Jon wanted to question the people who had booths near the curtain. Those exhibitors had been briefly interviewed by campus cops yesterday; now it was necessary to follow up.

I stayed behind Hopkins in an attempt to watch his reactions. He didn't seem to care that I was behind him; he didn't single me out for conversation. He seemed as he always had... cheerfully oblivious.

I didn't know what to think.

The romance aisle where I'd broken up the fight between Mercedes and Ruth Zwick was at the far left of the enormous floor of the Wooden Center, closest to the heavy curtain behind which Mercedes had been found. We entered the exhibit hall, turned left, and stopped at the first booth we came to, at the end of the sci-fi aisle. The guy there was the one who'd commented on the "catfight."

Kevin and Jon showed their badges and a picture of Mercedes, a printout of her driver's license photo. Kevin asked, "Have you ever seen this woman?"

The guy frowned at the picture. "Um - maybe? There were a couple of women fighting back there yesterday. I think that's one of them."

Jon removed his notepad and pen from his jacket pocket. "What's your name, sir?"

"Matt Tarver."

Jon made a note. "After that fight, did you see her again?"

"Naw. The cops kicked her out, right? I didn't see her after that."

"Okay, thanks." Jon handed the guy a card.

We turned away. Hopkins said, "One down."

Kevin sighed.

The woman at the end booth of the next aisle - the self-help section - didn't recognize Mercedes at all. Hopkins said, "Strike two."

Even Jon didn't respond to that.

The third aisle was populated by writers of military, government, and post-apocalyptic thrillers. The guy at the end booth had a table full of books with ominous covers, typically a federal government building starkly outlined against a red and black sky. He squinted at the photo of Mercedes that Jon held up. "Oh, her. Yeah, I was at the keynote speech yesterday. First time I'd ever seen her, though."

Kevin asked, "Had you heard of her before yesterday, Mister....?"

"Ross. Dan Ross. Sure, I'd heard of her." He smiled crookedly. "Most self-pubbed authors know the stars in the business. I've read about her in the newsletters."

Jon asked, "Know anyone who might want to kill her?"

Ross's eyes widened. "Damn. So the reports were true?"

Kevin said, "Afraid so."

"Well, to answer your question, no." Ross spread his hands. "I didn't know anything about her at all, other than her financial success." He snorted softly. "Romance. No accounting for taste, huh?"

Jon gave him a card, and we moved on.

Kevin said, "Here's the mystery aisle. Let's see if Testaverde has found his ice pick."

We didn't get far. The guy at the second booth in scurried around his table and stopped in front of us. "You gentlemen are homicide detectives, correct?"

The man was only about 5'6" and was dressed as a caricature of Hercule Poirot, right down to the mustache. A bowler hat was resting on top of a stack of boxes behind his table. Kevin said, "Who are you?"

The man bowed. "Arthur Bates, at your service. I am the creator of Clive Cross." His fake British accent grated on my ears.

He clearly expected us to know who that was. Jon said, "Clive Cross?"

Bates looked offended. "Yes. Former MI6 agent and master sleuth." He indicated the display of books at his table. "Surely you're familiar with my work."

Kevin said, "No. Sorry."

"No matter." Bates leaned forward. "I have a theory about your murder."

Jon's expression read, *This oughta be good.* Kevin crossed his arms. "What's that?"

Bates glanced around. No one was paying any attention to us, but he lowered his voice anyway. "Mercedes Moran was *poisoned.*"

Jon raised an eyebrow. Hopkins's forehead wrinkled in confusion. Kevin's expression was deadpan. "By whom?"

"Well. I've hardly had time to determine *that*, have I?"

Jon asked, "How did you know Ms. Moran?"

"Ah, er, I didn't. But I saw the report of her death on the news. Her skin tone indicated *immediately* to me that she suffered from silver poisoning."

Clearly, the manner of Mercedes's death hadn't been released to the public. Kevin said, "Silver poisoning, huh?"

"That's correct." He plucked a sheet of paper from his table and presented it to Kevin. "I've compiled a list of exhibitors from the Bay Area. You should find out which of them has access to colloidal silver."

"Uh huh." Kevin folded the paper neatly and slid it into his back pocket. "Mr. Bates?"

Bates drew himself up, seemingly expecting thanks or praise. "Yes?"

Kevin leaned down so his eyeballs were about six inches from Bates'. "Stay the hell out of my investigation, or I will put you in jail. Is that clear?"

Bates backed up. "*Well. I never.*"

Jon said, "Let me see your ID, Mr. Bates."

Bates spluttered, but he produced his driver's license. Jon recorded the details then handed it back. "Do the cops in Terre Haute consult with you on cases?"

"Er - no. Although I have offered my services."

"I bet you have." Jon clicked his pen closed. "Mr. Bates, the Los Angeles Police Department is not going to consult with you on this or *any* case. The penalty for interference with a police investigation in California is one year in jail and a $1,000 fine. I promise you - the Los Angeles Men's Central Jail is not a place you want to spend an hour, much less a year. Do we understand each other?"

Bates sulked. "Yes."

Jon smiled widely. "Wonderful. Have a nice day."

Bates huffily retreated behind his booth as we walked away. Hopkins waited until we were a few feet away then said, "Good job, Detective. That fella needed to have the facts of life explained to him."

Kevin shook his head in disgust. "Crime writers. They do a few hours of research, read a book on forensics, and think they know as much about investigation as we do."

Jon said, "A little knowledge is a dangerous thing."

Hopkins sighed. "Everyone's a critic."

Chapter 15
A Disgrace to His (Former) Profession

As we approached, we could see that Guy Testaverde wasn't at his booth. The display wall behind him was empty. I asked, "Where did the weapons go?"

Jon said, "We confiscated them. They're in our evidence locker."

Hopkins nodded sagely. "Better safe than sorry."

Kevin was looking over Hopkins's shoulder. "Here he comes. Jamie, make yourself scarce."

I crossed the aisle and pretended to be browsing through a stack of books at the booth opposite. Since I was the one who told Kevin about the ice pick, we thought it might be best if he didn't see me in the company of the cops.

The woman at the booth said, "Hi! Are you a mystery fan?"

"Um - yes." I gave her a quick smile.

Behind me Guy Testaverde said, "You'd better be here to tell me you found my ice pick."

A soft snort escaped me. The woman at the booth looked puzzled. "Are you searching for something specific?"

"Oh. Sorry, no. I'm eavesdropping." I tipped my head toward Testaverde's booth.

"Oh!" The woman gave me a thumbs up and went to speak to another loiterer.

Kevin said, "We'd prefer that *you* tell *us* that you found it."

Testaverde grunted. "It hasn't turned up. Who are you?"

Hopkins answered. "Lieutenant Nelson Hopkins. You dropped the ball on this one, Officer Testaverde."

"What?"

Hopkins sounded smug. "A little bird at the Tequesta Police Department told me that you removed the knives you had displayed from the evidence locker without permission. You're up the creek without a paddle, son."

Testaverde spluttered. "You *checked up* on me?"

Hopkins said, "That's how we do it in the City of Angels. I spoke to the Internal Affairs officer at TPD. He's on his way here to retrieve the department's evidence and have a little heart-to-heart with you. If I can make a suggestion - honesty is the best policy."

I grinned. Hopkins's IAG skills were coming in handy.

Testaverde said, "But…"

Hopkins said, "Now, son, let me give you some friendly advice. When you find yourself in a hole, stop digging."

Testaverde got blustery. "If *you* people were doing your jobs…"

Hopkins's voice held a note of warning. "Whoa, there, Nellie. Don't even go there."

Kevin said, "The only reason we haven't arrested you for Mercedes Moran's murder is that we don't have enough evidence yet. But if you killed her, we'll find out."

"There *is* no evidence because I *didn't* kill her."

Jon said, "Maybe not. But if you supplied the murder weapon, you're an accessory before the fact."

"But…"

Hopkins said, "Now, son. Don't get your panties in a twist. We don't intend to lock you up and throw away the key without cause. But until we find either your ice pick or our killer, whichever comes first, we expect you to be at our beck and call. Let me make this simple for you. *Don't. Leave. Town.*"

A male voice I didn't recognize said, "Uh - hi? Mr. Testaverde? Are you signing books today?"

Hopkins said, "He's all yours, son."

I heard Kevin, Jon and Hopkins move away. I waited for a few seconds, until Testaverde was engaged with his fan, and followed them.

When I caught up, Jon was chuckling. I kept my voice down. "Did you all *plan* that?"

Jon said, "Nope. The good lieutenant took it upon himself to contact the TPD."

Hopkins grinned at me. "I figured it couldn't hurt to hold his feet to the fire. As it happens, Mr. Testaverde has been a thorn in the side of the boys in blue in Tequesta for a month of Sundays. Their Internal Affairs officer wasn't surprised to hear from me."

Kevin said, "We were going to call them as soon as we finished here. There's no way they'd release those knives, even if the cases were solved."

Hopkins slapped Kevin on the shoulder. "And you were right on the money, son."

I said, "He had an accomplice in the department, right?

Hopkins nodded. "Another bad actor, who'd already been kicked downstairs to the lowest link on the food chain."

Jon said, "The property room?"

"Got it in one."

I said, "I hope his former department will give him more than a slap on the wrist."

Kevin said, "They ought to take away his pension."

Hopkins said, "He made his bed. Now he's got to lie in it."

The other interviews in the exhibit hall didn't generate any leads. At the end of the room, we stepped behind the heavy red curtain that had shielded Mercedes's final moments from view. The floor had been cleaned. Other than several rows of folding chairs, the space was empty.

Kevin walked to the spot where Mercedes had been found and stopped, his hands on his hips, listening. Jon ambled slowly along the curtain, also listening. After a minute Kevin said, "It's considerably quieter back here. Sound would be muffled in both directions."

Hopkins said, "No one out front would hear our damsel in distress."

Jon said, "Not unless she was shouting."

Kevin sighed deeply and rubbed his eyes. "Okay. The conference organizers should have the list of attendees for us. We need to get that, then call in Elias and Jill."

Jon pulled out his phone. "I'll text Kristen, see if she has any names for us yet."

Hopkins checked his watch. "Do you boys plan to chow down at some point? Man does not live by coffee alone."

Jon said, "Yes, sir, but we'll have to eat on the fly today."

"Ah, yes. As police officers have done from time immemorial."

We returned to the hubbub of the exhibit hall and made our way toward the exit. When we reached the restrooms, Hopkins said, "I need to make a pit stop, boys. Don't go anywhere without me." He darted into the men's room.

I said, "I'm meeting Pete for lunch, then there's a conference session that I have to attend. I must bid you a fond farewell. Parting is such sweet sorrow."

Kevin growled. "Shut. Up. Please."

"Well, since you asked nicely…"

Jon said, "*Someone* got up on the wrong side of the bed this morning."

Kevin glared at Jon. "It's a good thing you're cute."

Chapter 16
Clouds On the Horizon

I walked into Westwood, to 800 Degrees, to meet Pete, Christine and Andy. By the time I arrived, they had already ordered. I placed my own order and joined them at the table. "I guess Sam is busy elsewhere."

Andy said, "Yeah. There's a reception at the LGBT center, then a meeting of the Earth Science student organization."

Pete said, "It's great that she's getting involved so quickly."

Chris looked concerned. "I just hope it's not too much. She needs to concentrate on her classes."

I said, "It'll be fine. She'll make friends at the LGBT center, and the Earth Science organization will keep her focused on her degree."

Pete said, "When I came to UCLA, I was fortunate to be on the baseball team. It's such a big school - if you don't get connected, you can get lost."

I said, "Kristen and I met Sam's roommate yesterday. Ysabel. She's a science major, too, so with luck they'll support each other's study habits."

Andy said, "I hope so. We took Ysabel to dinner with us last night. She said her parents expect her to come home every weekend."

Pete asked, "Why?"

"She was vague on the subject, but it sounded to me like they might be - er - controlling."

Pete frowned. "That doesn't sound promising."

Chris said, "If she's gone, though, Sam will have plenty of peace and quiet to study."

"I mean for Ysabel. Kids of controlling parents sometimes go wild in college."

I said, "If they're that controlling, why didn't they make her go to UCSD? Their marine biology program is better than ours."

Andy said, "We didn't ask."

Chris said, "She's *extremely* forthcoming. She announced her asexuality to us almost before we'd been seated."

I said, "Yeah, she told Kristen and me the same thing. I *was* surprised that she was so open with people she'd just met. But I'm glad that Sam is rooming with someone who's something other than straight."

Pete said, "And if Ysabel is truly ace, she likely won't be sneaking anyone into the room for sex. Another bonus for Sam."

Chris said, "I suppose. I just don't want to see Sam get sucked into anyone else's drama."

I chuckled. "I hate to tell you, Chris, but if you live in campus housing, that's inevitable."

Pete said, "Sam can always escape to us if she needs to."

Chapter 17
Vicious Rumors

I said goodbye to Chris and Andy - they were driving home tomorrow, and I wouldn't see them again before they left - and went back to campus. The afternoon conference sessions on nonfiction writing and publishing were set to begin at 1:30. I found the designated room at Carnesale Commons, snagged a back row seat and texted Kristen. *In place for the nonfiction publishing session. Whatcha doing?*

Reading Mercedes Moran's blog. OMFG.

Nasty?

The only surprise is that it took someone this long to kill her.

Uh oh. You making a list of names?

Yep.

I texted Kevin next. *Back at the conference. What's new?*

In the process of calling the contacts on Moran's phone. There aren't many. Spoke to her attorney, who tried his best to implicate Martie Pepper.

Not surprising. What's Hopkins doing?

Following us around like a little kid.

Still think he might be checking up on me?

Maybe not. He hasn't asked us anything about you.

Jeez, thanks for scaring me for NO reason.

Doesn't mean he isn't.

I sent a tongue-sticking-out emoji, then a thought occurred to me. *Several women in the crowd recorded the fight between Mercedes and Ruth Zwick on their phones. You should get the videos.*

Oh, brilliant. Have to figure out how to do that…

Good. My session's starting. See ya.

What time are you done?

3:30.

Meet us at library after.

OK.

I opened an email to myself, intending to take notes as I listened. The session was a panel discussion. I searched for the affiliations of the participants and discovered that they weren't connected to academic institutions. Of the four panelists, three only listed the books they'd written as credentials. The other one was retired from the U.S. Army.

As I feared, the discussion wasn't useful to me. One speaker focused on the importance of fact checking and footnotes when writing nonfiction and suggested cultivating a relationship with a librarian.

Couldn't argue with that.

One of the speakers talked about marketing and search engine optimization and the use of Amazon's categories and keywords to make a book climb the bestseller list. Another spoke on the importance of professional editing and cover art. The fourth discussed possible methods of attracting publishers once the work was self-published and which publishers should be avoided.

I sighed and cancelled the email to myself without writing a word. In terms of collection development for the library, there was no way to know whether a self-published nonfiction book was worth buying unless we had read it ourselves.

In terms of writing, I couldn't think of a single subject that I felt passionately enough about that I'd self-publish if all else failed. Besides, if I hadn't had my editor David Beaton and the prestige and resources of Oxford University Press behind me, I'd never have been awarded a sabbatical.

In terms of academic scholarship, I doubted whether a self-published book would carry the same weight with a promotion committee as a traditionally published one. I was sympathetic with the plight of the self-published nonfiction author, but I didn't see how their books were going to have much impact on research libraries. There wasn't a system in place to bring the two arenas together.

At least I'd have that to report to Dr. Madorsky.

I didn't want to be rude by leaving before the discussion ended, so I texted Pete. *Chris and Andy still with you?*

No, they went to Kristen's to swim. I'm at home. Where are you?

At the conference. Ugh.

Not learning anything?

Learning that quality self-published nonfiction will be difficult to identify re: collection development. Only discoverable by accident.

Logical. How are you going to solve a romance author's murder, sitting in a discussion about nonfiction?

Ha. Meeting with the cops when this is over.

I decided that I'd wait to ask Pete about Kevin's theory - that Hopkins was watching me - in person.

The session ended at 3:15. I was on my way out of the building when I saw the three *Fast and Furious* fans who'd stopped me yesterday. I ducked to the side of the hallway to avoid them, but failed. They spotted me and made a beeline in my direction.

The one who I thought was named Danielle said, "Thank God. We've been looking for you *everywhere*."

I held up my hand. "I thought we had this misunderstanding sorted."

"Oh, no, it's not about *that*." She pointed to herself. "I'm Danielle, this is Heather, and this is Winter."

I shook their hands. "I'm Jamie, remember?"

Danielle huffed a little. "*Yes*, we remember. But listen. You're working with the cops, right? We have some information about Mercedes Moran's death."

Heather said, "I wouldn't call it *information*. I'd call it speculation."

Danielle rolled her eyes. "Fine, but where there's smoke, there's fire, right?"

I considered asking Danielle if her last name was Hopkins. "What have you heard?"

Winter said, "We should start at the beginning. The three of us - we're here because we write fanfiction, and we want to switch to *actual* fiction so we can publish. Make some money, you know?"

Danielle said, "We spent all morning in sessions about copyright. Anyway. We were hanging out with some people in the fanfiction community, and one of them started talking trash about Mercedes."

"Talking trash how?"

"Calling her a tranny. Saying she wasn't a woman at all. Saying *terrible* things about her, like she deserved to die. He was *angry*."

Heather said, "If you know anything about fanfiction, you know that we're an open-minded group. It took us a minute to react because we were so stunned."

I said, "Mercedes began her career by writing fanfiction. Is she well known in the community?"

Winter said, "Oh, yeah. *Everyone* knows her. She's the career model we all aspire to."

"Do you know this guy? His name?"

Danielle said, "His name is Cody Muñoz. He writes *Miami Vice* fanfiction. Violent stuff."

I wondered if there was a connection between Cody and Guy Testaverde. "And he's registered at the conference?"

Heather said, "Yes. He's staying at the same hotel as us."

I made a note in my phone. *Cody Muñoz. Royal Palace Westwood.* "I'll pass this on. Thanks, ladies."

Danielle said, "Just doing our civic duty."

"Right. Listen, don't confront this guy. If he has violent tendencies, you don't want to mess with him."

The women agreed. I said, "Why does Cody think that Mercedes was a trans woman? Does he have any evidence for that?"

Winter snorted. "No. He just thinks she looks like a man. Any woman that doesn't conform to his idea of femininity either has to be 'a tranny' or 'a lezzy.'" Her air quotes expressed her disgust.

"Lovely. Okay, thanks again. I'm going to see the cops right now."

I left to a chorus of goodbyes.

Chapter 18
Meanwhile, Back At the Ranch...

When I got back to the library, I texted Kevin. *Where are you?*
Your first floor conference room.

The conference room had been converted into an impromptu
command post. A coffee machine had been appropriated from
somewhere and was gurgling away in the corner, filling a fresh pot.
Kevin and Jon were hunched over laptops; Elias Pinter was on the
phone, and Jill Branigan was poring over a lengthy printout.
Lieutenant Hopkins was at the far end of the table, sipping coffee.
When he saw me, he saluted me with his coffee cup. "Dr. Brodie!
Fancy meeting you here! Take a load off."

Kevin grimaced without raising his head. I dropped into the seat
beside Jill. "What's going on?"

"Kristen is in her office reading the victim's blog. She's created
and has shared with all of us a spreadsheet of names of potential
suspects and as much information about them as she can dig out.
There are over a *hundred* names so far. Kevin and Jon are running
background on the names. We're checking them against this list" -
she indicated the printout - "to see if they're attending the
conference. If they are, or if they're local, Elias and I will track 'em
down and interview them. If they're not in town, we'll call them."

I told Jill about my encounter with Danielle et al. "Do you have
the name Cody Muñoz on your spreadsheet?"

Jill checked. "No. But I think we'd better have a conversation
with him before any of these."

Elias ended his call. "Tim says to send him the names and
numbers of the out-of-towners. He'll call them himself."

I said, "Is he well enough to do that?"

"He says so. He wanted to come back to work today, but his
doctor wouldn't release him. He says he's going stir-crazy at home."

I whispered, "What's the lieutenant doing?"

Jill whispered back. "Observing. It's creepy."

I said, more loudly, "What can I do?" If Hopkins was watching
me, I'd give him something to watch.

Kevin looked up. "Stella Kim is still at the law library, isn't
she?"

"Yes."

"Ask her to find any and all court documents she can relating to Mercedes Moran and Tammy Thomas. I know how to do that but I don't have time."

"Okay. I'll walk over there. It'll be easier to explain in person." Not really, but I needed the exercise.

Jon said, "If it's an absolute must."

I said, "It'd be a pain in the neck to handle via email."

Hopkins said, "We can't let anything fall through the cracks. Go dot the I's and cross the T's, Dr. Brodie. We're in a race against time here."

Elias chuckled. Jill just shook her head. I said, "Right, sir. I won't let the grass grow under my feet."

Kevin muttered, "Oh, for God's sake…"

I darted out the door before he threw something at me.

Stella Kim was one of my friend Melanie Hayes's law school classmates. She spent a couple of years in the public defender's office, couldn't take it anymore and went to library school where she was in the class ahead of me.

Fortunately, I located her in her office. She looked up in surprise. "Hey, Jamie! Haven't seen you for a while."

"I know. How's everything here?"

She waved her hand in a dismissive gesture. "SS, DD. What's up?"

"I need every court document ever filed about one particular person. Can you do that?"

"Is it a California resident?"

"Yep."

"Then the answer is yes." She picked up a pen. "What's the name?"

"Originally, Tammy Thomas. As of eight years ago, Mercedes Moran."

"Why the name change?"

"Career move, we think. She lived in San Jose as Thomas and in San Francisco as Moran. She was the woman killed over at the Wooden Center, at that conference."

"Okay." Stella wrote down the names and locations. "Shall I send this to you?"

"No, send it to Kevin." I recited his email address.

"Will do. He's still working for Mel, isn't he?"

"Yeah, a few hours a week. But he doesn't have time to do this himself."

"Got it. I'll start now."

"Thanks, Stella."

On the way back to the conference room I swung by Kristen's office. She was chewing on the cap of a pen, scrolling with her mouse. I said, "Still with the blog?"

"Yeah." She checked the time. "For another hour, at least."

"Want anything?"

She brightened. "Tea would be wonderful."

I bowed. "Your wish is my command."

She snickered. "Kevin's ready to disown us all."

I went to Café 451 and got a large cup of black tea, took it to Kristen and returned to the conference room. Elias and Jill were gone. I said, "Stella's on it. She'll email you what she finds."

"Okay, thanks." Kevin rubbed the back of his neck.

"Anything else you need from me?"

Jon checked the time. "Don't think so. It's about time for you to leave, right?"

"Yeah, but I could…"

Hopkins held up his hand. "Now, son, don't be a glutton for punishment. We appreciate the goodwill gesture, but you're a civilian. You go on and hit the road."

I said, "Yes, sir. You don't have to tell me twice."

Jon grinned. Kevin sighed deeply. "You'll call Dad tonight, right?"

Dad's first date with Claudia Stratton, a woman he met on Sunday at the Dodgers-Padres game and chatted with throughout, had been scheduled for lunchtime today. "Yeah. I'll let you know what he says."

Jon said, "We'll still be here, burning the midnight oil."

I opened my mouth, intending to say, *There's no rest for the weary*, and Kevin froze me with a look. He said, "Please leave."

"Yes, *sir*. Good night, Lieutenant Hopkins."

Hopkins saluted me. "See you tomorrow, Dr. Brodie. It'll be another day of action-packed adventure."

Chapter 19
Love Is In the Air?

I updated Pete on Mercedes Moran over dinner. He gave me a sly grin. "They're searching for a needle in a haystack."

I laughed. "Poor Kevin."

"They still don't know why Hopkins is there?"

"Well - they have a theory." I explained.

Pete burst out laughing. "They're really grasping at straws, aren't they?"

"Excellent cliché placement there, but why is that idea so funny?"

"A, if IAG was interested in you, you'd *know*. B, they wouldn't have waited this long to investigate you. That's the best Kev and Jon can do?"

I sighed. "Yeah. Their captain said to not ask questions. Jill Branigan said he's just watching them. She said it was creepy."

"I'm sure." Pete looked mystified. "I can't imagine why he's there."

"If he was investigating Kevin or Jon, *they'd* know, right?"

"Without a doubt."

"There's no way he's polishing his homicide investigative skills, is there?"

He snorted in derision. "That would be *no*."

After dinner, I couldn't stand the suspense any longer. I texted Dad - *You free to talk?*

His response was to call me. "Hey, sport. I guess I know what you're gonna ask me."

I chuckled. "You're right. How did your date with Claudia go?"

"It was fantastic. We had lunch and talked for a couple of hours, then walked to the beach and talked some more."

"Wow. What did you talk about?"

"Baseball, dogs, her career, my career, you guys… What it was like to suddenly lose a spouse who you intended to have many more years with."

"*Oh*." My mom was killed by a drunk driver when I was six months old. To my knowledge, Dad had never discussed his feelings about that with *anyone*. "How long had she been married when her husband died?"

"Eight years, same as Julie and me. It was eighteen years ago. Her husband taught chemistry at Caltech. Died of a heart attack during a faculty meeting."

"That's awful. She must have married at an older age than you."

"Right. She didn't get married until she was 36."

I did some quick math. "So she's 62? She looks younger."

I could hear the grin in my dad's voice. "She does, doesn't she?"

"When are you seeing her again?"

"Friday... for dinner. On Saturday we're going with Jeff and the boys to the Padres-Giants game."

"Oooh, so Jeff will get to meet her."

"Yep." He hesitated a moment. "Do you think I'm moving too fast?"

"Hell, no. What's too fast? You like her, she likes you, and you have similar interests - why not go for it? If she thinks you're moving too fast, she'll say so. She didn't strike me as being one to agree to anything she didn't want to do."

"True. And the baseball game was her idea."

"Well. There you go. You should bring her hiking soon. See how she holds up in the mountains."

Dad chuckled. "She appears fit to me. Are you hiking this weekend?"

I sighed. "Probably not. Kev, Kristen and I are tangled up in another murder case." I gave him a brief outline of the Mercedes Moran tale.

"Ah. Maybe next weekend, then. But we'll see you at Neil's party on Sunday." My dad's friend and ours, Neil Anderson, was celebrating his birthday this weekend.

"Right. Have fun Friday night. But not *too* much fun."

He just laughed.

Pete looked up, smiling, when I ended the call. "Sounds like it went well. They're going out Friday night?"

"Dinner on Friday, baseball on Saturday with Jeff and the kids."

"It'll be interesting to see what Jeff thinks of her, since he remembers your mom."

"He *barely* remembers her. You don't think he'll react badly, do you? He never did to Barb." Barb Simmons, my dad's former girlfriend.

"I think he knew that Dave and Barb weren't going anywhere. If your dad gets serious with Claudia - I just wonder how Jeff will react."

I frowned. "I'd hope he'd be *thrilled* for Dad."

Pete turned his attention back to his laptop. "Yeah. You'd hope."

I texted Kevin. *Dad's date was, in his words, fantastic. They're having dinner Friday and she's meeting Jeff and Colin Saturday. You home yet?*

No. Hopkins left and we came back to the station to put the murder book together and organize these interviews. Capt. approved OT so might as well get it over with.

Did you find Cody Muñoz?

Yes. Homophobic, transphobic, misogynistic, steaming pile of shit. He's in an interview room right now. Elias and I are gonna put the fear of God in him.

If he's a bully, he's a coward. Might also be queer and in denial.

Sure. We'll keep that in mind.

Chapter 20
Nothing to See Here, Folks, Move Along

I joined Pete on the sofa and he closed his laptop with a sigh. I asked, "Do you have grading?"

"I can do it tomorrow. Where did you leave that book the Florida cop gave you?"

"Um - it's upstairs. Do you want to read it?"

"Yeah. I'm curious."

I retrieved the book and brought it to Pete. He examined the cover, shaking his head. "Very *Miami Vice*, isn't it?"

"That's practically historical fiction."

"Mm hm." He turned the book over, where Guy Testaverde's visage, bearing a tough-guy expression, was displayed over a blurb. Pete read, "'Ridge Carson' - where do authors get these names? - 'is a rogue cop. He needs a big score to get his badge back. Rico Sanchez' - of *course* the bad guy has to be Hispanic - 'is the drug kingpin of South Florida. Rico knows Ridge is coming for him, and he has a few surprises waiting.

'But Ridge doesn't play by the rules... and he has a few surprises of his own for Rico.'" Pete dropped his head to the back of the sofa and groaned. "Oh my *God*."

"Are you sure you want to read this?"

"No." Pete opened the book and flipped a few pages. "Here's the dedication. 'To my brothers and sisters in blue.' Big of him to include the sisters."

I poked his shoulder. "Come on, get to the good stuff."

"Okay." He turned to Chapter 1, and we began to read.

The sun rose heavy that morning, hovering over Biscayne Bay like a big red balloon, or the big orange ball at a Union 76 station.

I said, "He took a writing class once, and all he remembers is that he's supposed to use similes."

Ridge Carson's alarm clock rang. The sound hit his ears like an anvil. He reached out and threw the thing across the room, knocking over the empty bottle of gin as he did.

Ridge staggered from the bed to the galley. He needed to piss but he needed aspirin worse. His head was pounding like a jackhammer.

Pete said, "Our hero lives on a boat."

I said, "I bet he has a pet alligator, too."

Ridge downed three aspirin with half a Bud. A hair of the dog couldn't hurt. He fired up the coffee maker and climbed to the deck. He forgot his shade's, and the molten sun seared his eyeballs like a hot iron.

I was laughing too hard to speak. Pete tossed the book onto the ottoman. "Every moment I spend reading this is a moment that I'll never get back. That's *awful*."

I managed to control myself. "Apostrophes R Us?"

"Seriously. I can't *imagine* his descriptions of police work."

"You should read more when you're in the mood. It's gotta be hilarious."

He scowled at the offending novel. "I don't want to ever be in the mood for *that*."

I retrieved the book and flipped through a few pages in the center. "Ooh, here's a two-page-long description of a sniper rifle."

Pete scanned the section I'd indicated, shaking his head. "I think he copied this from the specs manual." He turned to the end of the book and read for a minute. "And our hero gets his badge back as a reward for murdering the bad guy. Like that would *ever* happen."

"Maybe it would in Tequesta, Florida."

Pete made a sound of disgust. "And here's a sex scene with the requisite big-bosomed babe. Ugh." He tossed the book back to the ottoman. "This is cop porn. There's a segment of the law enforcement population that dreams itself capable of this variety of garbage. I bet ol' Guy has quite a following."

"Well, as Lieutenant Hopkins would say, there's no accounting for taste."

Thursday, September 28

Chapter 21
Covering All the Bases

On the bus the next morning, I was still chuckling about Guy Testaverde's book. I wondered if his ice pick had turned up yet, then had another idea. I texted Karen Lewis.

Hey, ever hear of a mystery-thriller writer named Guy Testaverde?

Yes. Why?

He has a booth at the conference and gave me a freebie. First book in his series. Read the first page and it's terrible. Just wondered if you knew of him.

I know of him because he's a poacher.

What??

He poaches spots on bestseller lists. Tags his books with categories he doesn't belong in, just to get onto as many lists as he can.

That's allowed?

Yep. Publishing companies do it, too. The author or publisher can choose two categories and seven tags for each book, and Amazon's bots assign the book to that category without checking that it's legit.

Unfair!

Yes. Complaining to Amazon is useless. I know it's been an issue for gay mystery as well.

Ugh. Hard to imagine he's on ANY bestseller lists.

Ha! He writes guns and babes. Popular in certain circles, apparently.

That's what Pete said. He hated it.

Pete is a wise man. You going to conference today?

Not until afternoon.

OK. Later.

I hoped to be able to work through the morning. Classes commenced today, and I didn't want to fall behind. There was a session at the publishing conference about libraries this afternoon which Kristen and I would be expected to attend. I had rugby practice again this evening and didn't want to have to handle work-related email after practice.

Pete and I had better things to do after practice.

But noooooo.

I'd no sooner logged into my computer, cyber-announcing my presence via Skype, than Kristen IM'ed me. *Need your help.*

With what?

Going through this social media crap. Mercedes was EVERYWHERE.

I groaned to myself. *It's like you said, I don't have accounts.*

You can use mine. I'm coming up there.

Bossy, aren't we?

Get used to it, little brother. :D

What's THAT supposed to mean?

But Kristen had already changed her status to "out of office." I sighed and opened a browser. When she appeared in my doorway a minute later, I said, "Little brother? Just exactly what are you implying?"

She grinned. "Not a thing. Can you stand reading tweets?"

"Better than Facebook posts. What about the blog?"

"I read the entire blog yesterday. It *took* the entire day between posts, comments and following links." She logged me into her Twitter account.

I said, "It just occurred to me... has Kevin objected to your social media presence? As soon as he was accepted to the police academy, he asked Dad, Jeff, Val and me to not open social media accounts."

"We've discussed it. I understand that he doesn't want to expose any of us to anyone he might arrest and all that. But I'm a digital communications librarian. I can't drop off social media. *But* I'm careful not to reveal anything. I've never posted photos of myself or the house and never mentioned Kevin's name. I mostly tweet library stuff, and I only use Facebook to keep up with my family."

"And he's okay with that?"

"Mostly." She grinned as she located Mercedes Moran's Twitter feed. "There you go. I'll search Facebook."

I sighed and began reading. Mercedes's final tweets had occurred just before and after her keynote speech on Tuesday. After the speech, she'd sent two tweets. One read, *Carmen Hidalgo, author of* Mercury's Rainbow? *IRL "Carmen" is Edna Brown. Not even a little bit Spanish. Sad!*

Her last tweet was, *SHOCKING discovery! "Angelica Ashley" of Rose Trilogy is a MAN! IRL Elmer Thrash. Big league FRAUD!*

Mercedes must have studied Tweeting 101 under the current POTUS. I looked at the time stamps, but each of them only said, *Sep 19*. Not helpful for establishing a timeline before Mercedes's death.

Before her speech Mercedes had tweeted, *About to give keynote at ASP conference. Stay tuned for MAJOR announcement!*

I showed it to Kristen. "The major announcement was her exposé of Angelica Ashley."

"Unless she had something bigger planned and the fracas after Martie Pepper spoke kept her from it."

"What could have been bigger than uncovering Elmer Thrash?"

Kristen leaned her chin on her hand. "That's been bothering me. The idea is that she wants - wanted - to expose authors, right? But Elmer Thrash is dead. Who's she hurting by uncovering his identity?"

"Maybe she was trying to dissuade any more readers from buying the books, since Martie was suing her."

"No…" Kristen shook her finger at me. "She was going for media coverage. Only romance fans are likely to be aware of Mercedes. Everyone on the *planet* knows who Angelica Ashley is. Was. Sort of was."

I laughed. "I know what you mean."

"The Rose trilogy sold over 150 million copies. Was translated into more than fifty languages. Angelica was interviewed - not in person, of course - by every major media outlet in the *world*. I bet that Mercedes figured she could snag a chunk of notoriety by exposing Angelica. Elmer. Whoever."

"Any publicity is good publicity? Even if it pissed off 150 million of Angelica's readers?"

"Think about it. If even a million of those readers each bought a few of Mercedes's books, even if it was only out of curiosity - her net worth would *explode*. Mercedes herself would be interviewed by major news outlets. She might even receive an offer for film rights."

"Ugh." I leaned back in my chair. "That makes perfect sense, though. Far more than does Mercedes's outing of all these small-time authors who are sweet middle-aged ladies. I don't buy for a second that she was doing it because the reading public has the right to know."

Kristen said, "No. Her blog made it quite clear that Mercedes didn't give a rat's ass about the reading public, except in terms of them buying her books. I think she was stealing readers. Hoping that if someone was shocked enough that their Spanish princess was an Arkansas housewife, they'd quit reading the housewife's books and switch their loyalty to Mercedes."

"Her game backfired, didn't it?"

"Yep." Kristen tapped her laptop screen. "And the answer has to be in here somewhere."

I sighed. "What if we find something? Take a screenshot?"

"Yeah. That way if it gets taken down, we'll have a record of it. And -" She turned to her laptop and clicked a few times. "I just shared a Google Sheet with you, the same one the police have, with a list of names of people she's outed or argued with. Most of the names were probably on the blog, but someone may have replied to a tweet who never saw her blog. The names are in alphabetical order on the sheet, so you can check to see if I've already added it."

"Yes, ma'am." I began to read.

Over two hours later, I'd finished my scrutiny of Mercedes Moran's Twitter feed, had searched the site using her name, and hadn't generated any new suspects. I said to Kristen, "All the names I came across were already on your list. I bet her blog is her primary outing tool."

"You're probably right. Want to check Goodreads next? There's a better chance of finding something there. More comments and reviews."

I sighed. "I guess. I don't have an account there either."

"What kind of librarian *are* you? No Goodreads account?"

I gave her a dirty look. "Just log me in already."

Mercedes's Twitter account had been straightforward. Her Goodreads account was nearly overwhelming. There were hundreds of reviews for each of her 82 books, plus an author Q and A section and a discussion board. I said, "*Damn.* I'll never get through this."

Kristen glanced at my screen. "Start with the discussion board. I'm almost done with Facebook, then I'll take the reviews and Q and A."

"How many people did Jon and Kevin have time to check yesterday?"

"They got the background work done on all of the blog names. Tim's called everyone on the list who didn't attend the conference and has ruled all of them out. Jill and Elias are on campus somewhere, tracking down and questioning the people named in the blog who are at the conference, and hunting down the owners of the additional names as you and I add them."

My perusal of the Goodreads discussion boards didn't add any new names to the list - for one thing, almost all Goodreads members used screen aliases - but it did uncover several heated arguments about Mercedes's activities. Some of the name-calling and accusations had gone on for days. Trying to capture all of them in screenshots wouldn't have preserved the continuity, so I printed them out.

By the time I clicked on the last topic, it was nearly lunchtime. I hoped to skim this one quickly - I was hungry - but was drawn up short when a name caught my eye.

Guy Testaverde.

I went back to the top of the discussion thread, labeled *Need Your Help!* The first post was from Mercedes herself, back in the spring.

Mercedes Moran: Readers, I need your help. We have a POACHER on the romance bestseller list!

MoranFan: A poacher? What's that?

Mercedes Moran: Someone who labels his books - HIS, in this case - as romance when they are clearly NOT. He's stealing spots on the bestseller lists from TRUE romance writers.

FanOfMoran: What's his genre?

Mercedes Moran: Police procedural.

MoranFan: Yuck!

MoranNumberOne: What can we do?

Mercedes Moran: Spread the word. Blog and tweet about him and his despicable practices. Leave bad reviews for his books. Email Amazon etc. with complaints.

FanOfMoran: We're on it!

MoranNumberOne: He won't know what hit him.

I said, "Kristen, read this one."

She leaned over to see my monitor. "Guy Testaverde? The ex-cop we met?"

"Yeah. Did Kevin tell you his ice pick went missing?"

"Oooh. No, but I've barely seen Kev this week. Print that one out."

The printer to which my computer was networked was in the East Asian Library, down the hall and around the corner. I was just standing up to collect my printing when Liz appeared, bearing a thick sheaf of paper. "These are from Goodreads and mention Mercedes Moran. I assume they're yours."

"Yes. Thank you." I reached out to take the stack from her.

She pulled it back. "Nunh unh. I didn't go to the printer for *you*. There's an article in here somewhere that I printed out."

Kristen snickered. I said, "Oops. Sorry. Here, I'll find it."

I flipped through the stack, found the twelve pages that were not like the others and handed them to Liz. "There you go. Undamaged."

"Thank you. Are you two gonna stop to eat lunch?"

Kristen said, "Of course. Just let me grab this one last screenshot... There." She closed her laptop. "Let's go."

Chapter 22
Opportunity Knocks

Samantha joined us for lunch, dumping a loaded backpack on the ground at her feet as she juggled a container of salad and a bottle of water. I asked, "How's it going so far?"

"Super. I've been in class since 8:00 this morning. Now I have all afternoon to study."

Liz asked, "You only took morning classes?"

"Yeah. I'm a morning person."

Kristen asked, "What are you taking?"

"Earth science, chemistry, English comp and calculus."

I whistled. "That's a pretty tough schedule."

"Nah." She grinned. "Except for calculus, I *love* all of those things."

Kristen said, "I predict great things for you, Sam."

Sam forked up a bite of salad. "That's the plan."

I asked, "What about Ysabel?"

"We don't have any classes together. She was still asleep when I left this morning."

Liz raised an eyebrow. I said, "She's *not* a morning person?"

"I guess not." Sam shrugged. "Just because we're roommates doesn't mean we have to hang out all the time, right?"

I said, "Right. As long as she's not awake at night wanting to talk or watch TV when you're trying to study or sleep."

Sam waved that off. "I'm going to study in the libraries. It'll be fine."

"Remember, you can always come to our house if you need peace and quiet."

"I *know*." Sam gave me a look that said, *You're being a stodgy uncle*. "It'll be *fine*."

I hoped so.

"Oh. I almost forgot." Sam reached into her backpack and produced a business card. "Would you take that to Uncle Pete, please?"

"Sure." I read the card. *Sadie Greer, Director, UCLA LGBTQ Center*. "What's this about?"

"There's a position available for a part-time campus counselor. It's only four hours a week, but I thought Uncle Pete might be interested."

"Indeed he might." Pete had expressed interest in a college counseling position back in the spring. Maybe this was an opportunity to discover his true calling. "Did you tell him about it?"

"I didn't have the chance yet. But I'll text him this afternoon."

Chapter 23
A Shot In the Dark

After lunch, Sam and Liz entered the library - Katrina Johnson was covering my shift on the reference desk - and Kristen and I went to Carnesale Commons to meet Gina and Karen at the session for librarians. I'd left the conference program in my office and hadn't bothered to see what this session was about.

If I had, I would have stayed away. It was, as far as I was concerned, entirely geared toward public librarians - taking them through the intricacies of buying from the self-publishing sites. Gina took notes, but I was soon bored. I texted Kevin. *Any solid suspects yet?*

Only Guy Testaverde. Everyone who publicly hated MM, including Cody Muñoz, has an alibi. Almost no one at this conference has been alone at any time.

Did you scare Muñoz?

Yup. You were right, he's a coward. Apparently 100% straight, just a bully. Elias made him cry.

Boo hoo. How goes the cliche-fest?

OMG. This case is a tough nut to crack. These writers come from all walks of life and all over the map. Hopkins wonders if any of these books are a must read. The social media information gives us more bang for our buck. Shall I go on?

Please don't. Still no idea why he's with you?

None.

Are you on campus?

No. On the way downtown to watch Moran's autopsy.

Ah. Are you having fun yet?

STFU. What do you know about the copyright office?

I paused for a second. The copyright office?? I typed, *It's part of Library of Congress. Why?*

Finished background on all of Moran's phone contacts. One works in IT at copyright office. Muriel Forsythe. Would she have access to authors' real names?

Ooooh, she might. Have you contacted her?

Called and left voice mail. No answer yet.

You could sic Blair on her. Our cousin Tyler's husband, Blair, was an archivist at the Library of Congress.

Oh, please. I'll sic the DC police on her first.

I laughed quietly. A woman at the front of the room was droning on about something. Kristen whispered, "What are you doing?"

"Entertaining myself. Shh."

She stuck her tongue out at me and turned her attention back to the speaker. I texted Pete, but he was walking Ammo and couldn't carry on a conversation. I tried my dad next. *What are you doing?*

Hi Uncle Jamie, it's Gabe. Grampa is driving.

Oh, OK. How's it going?

Fine. Grampa says do you need something?

Tell him no. I'll talk to him later.

OK.

I pocketed my phone with a sigh.

When Pete picked me up for rugby practice, I handed Sadie Greer's card to him. "Did Sam text you about this?"

"Yeah. It's intriguing." Pete glanced at the card, then set it in the cup holder and pulled away from the curb.

"Last spring when Elliott said he might become a college counselor, you thought it sounded intriguing then." Elliott Conklin was the assistant chair of the psychology department at Santa Monica College, Pete's former workplace.

Pete nodded. "I'll see what Sadie Greer says - but this could be a way to decide whether it's a fit for me."

"If it is, and this turns into a long-term gig, you could quit teaching."

Pete chuckled. "I just *started* teaching. Let's not rush out of anything."

"No, I don't mean that. I mean eventually."

"I know. If nothing else, it would be an attractive addition to my CV. Did you see Kevin and Jon today?"

"No, they went to Mercedes's autopsy. He did tell me by text that they had no fresh suspects yet."

Pete frowned. "I suppose Moran's murder could have nothing to do with the conference."

"Yeah - but isn't that unlikely? Nearly everyone that hated her is here."

"You're probably right." Pete drummed his fingers on the steering wheel, thinking. "What if the motive wasn't revenge for an outing? What if it was a preventive strike?"

I considered that. "Okay, it makes sense. But how would the killer know ahead of time that Mercedes was going to out her? Or him?"

He shook his head. "Beats me."

On the way home from rugby practice, I texted Kevin. *Autopsy results?*

Moran fought with someone. Skin under fingernails so DNA in the works. Also some bruising on neck, maybe consistent with someone using her scarf to try strangulation first. But bruises were a few hours older than stab wound.

She had two fights?

Maybe altercation before keynote speech, then attacker came back to finish the job? Pure speculation at this point.

Was it an ice pick?

Consistent with ice pick. Doesn't rule out something similar with same shape.

You home yet?

No, LAX. About to board flight to SFO. Need to search Moran's apartment. Also located a former coworker at programming job. Interview first thing in AM.

Back tomorrow? Barring any unforeseen circumstances, that is? :P

Shut up. Y, midafternoon.

Hopkins going with you?

Thank god no! Better go, time to board.

All systems are go? Bag and baggage on board? :P

ARGH. GOING TO AIRPLANE MODE NOW.

Friday, September 29

Chapter 23
Details Are Sketchy

Pete had emailed Sadie Greer while I was on the rugby pitch last night and wasn't expecting to hear from her before morning. But right before we'd gone to bed, she'd emailed back. *So pleased to hear that you're interested! Can you interview at 9:00 tomorrow morning?*

He'd responded in the affirmative. This morning he'd dressed in one of his better polo shirts and pressed trousers and we'd driven to work. As we exited the parking structure, he asked, "Are you going to the conference today?"

"There's one more session this morning, then I'm finished. Classes have started, and I *must* get some work done. See you at lunch?"

"Yep."

"Good luck with the interview."

"Thanks."

The morning session was a panel discussion by several publishers. It didn't start until 10:00. I dealt with email, then decided to take one more swing through the conference exhibits. On my way out of the building, I stopped at Kristen's office. "Hey. You going to any sessions today?"

"No." She waved her hand at her computer. "My civic duty comes first."

There was nothing new to see in the exhibit hall except that Guy Testaverde's booth was empty, the pegboard, books, and Guy himself having disappeared. The crowd was energetic and noisy. Mercedes Moran was apparently a distant memory. I didn't see anyone that appeared to be in mourning.

I found the room for the publisher discussion and took a seat. As other attendees filed in, I examined the rest of the conference schedule. There were sessions all day tomorrow and a closing keynote on Sunday morning by a self-published writer who'd attracted the attention of a mainstream publisher and was now on the *real* bestseller list - that of the *New York Times*.

I wasn't going to waste any of my weekend on this conference. I'd have to find out if Gina or Karen planned to attend.

The publishers' discussion was not relevant to libraries. The "publishers" on the panel turned out to be the pay-to-publish variety that made authors pay up front to see their books in print and provided almost nothing in return. I felt sorry for anyone who'd been suckered into that.

The panelists droned on. I took out my phone and began to play Spider Solitaire.

When the session ended, I pocketed my phone and headed back to the library, stopping by Powell on the way. Gina was at the reference desk and grinned when she saw me. "Why aren't you at the conference?"

"I just came from there. Why aren't you?"

"I'm going back this afternoon. We couldn't rearrange my reference shift today." She lowered her voice. "You're not going to any of the weekend sessions, are you?"

"Nope."

"Me either. Frida Nava told me that Dr. Madorsky is out of town this weekend. She'll never know."

I said, "As long as we have *something* to report to her, she won't care how many of the sessions we missed."

"Are you going to write up anything for her?"

"I don't have much to write up. Maybe we should produce a group report."

She pointed at me. "Fabulous idea. I'll start a Google Doc."

By the time I got back to the library, it was nearly noon. I let myself into Liz's office to get my lunch from her fridge and headed outside. When I got to our table, Pete was already there, talking to Liz and Kristen. I sat down and said, "How did it go with Sadie Greer?"

Pete grinned. "She hired me on the spot, and I got all the paperwork done at HR thanks to my transcripts being here. I start a week from Monday."

"Wow! What will your schedule be?"

"Late afternoon, 3:00 to 5:00 Tuesday and Thursday. I'll drive in and we can have dinner on campus then go straight to rugby after."

Liz said, "What's going on with the conference?"

Kristen said, "I'm too busy searching the internet for Mercedes Moran's enemies. I don't have time to sit through panel discussions on useless topics."

I said, "I'm done with it. This morning I went to a publisher presentation that turned out to be a bunch of vanity publishers. Completely worthless."

Kristen said, "Karen Lewis said she's going to the final keynote on Sunday."

"Good. Then none of the rest of us have to."

Liz said, "I hope the guys can get this case wrapped up by Sunday. I'd appreciate having at least one weekend day where Jon was free."

Kristen said, "No kidding."

Chapter 24
Tricks of the Trade

We had about fifteen minutes left in our shift when Kevin and Jon appeared, Hopkins trailing in their wake. Hopkins beamed when he saw us. "Dr. Brodie! Hard at work, eh? You're an inspiration to us all. And who is this lovely young lady?"

Liz held her hand out. "Hello, Lieutenant Hopkins. I'm Liz Nguyen, AKA Jon's wife."

Hopkins bowed formally over Liz's hand. "Ms. Nguyen, it is an honor to meet you." He nudged Jon. "Pretty as a picture, isn't she?"

Jon grinned. "A sight for sore eyes."

I figured I'd better rescue Kevin before the situation deteriorated. "What happened in San Francisco?"

Kevin said, "We searched Moran's apartment and brought her computers back with us. Our tech guys are trying to break the passwords now. The interview with her former coworker was…" He glanced around at the students in the area. "We'll tell you someplace more private."

Liz asked, "Did you finish the campus interviews?"

Kevin said, "Jill and Elias did that for us this morning. Nothing pertinent came of them."

Jon said, "That's all she wrote."

Kevin said, "We did get a break, though. Campus housekeeping found Mercedes Moran's missing scarf late last night."

Liz said, "Where?"

I said, "Are you sure it's hers?"

Jon said, "They found it stuffed inside a bunch of folding chairs in the Wooden Center. We know it's hers because we got photos of the opening session from the campus events coordinator."

Kevin said, "SID is examining it now for trace. We should have preliminary results by Monday. If someone tried to strangle her with it, their skin cells may be on it."

Hopkins said, "A ray of sunshine in this otherwise murky case."

Liz made a small sound of amusement.

I asked, "Did you ever watch any video of the fight?"

Jon, Kevin and Hopkins all looked at me. Hopkins said, "Video?"

"The day that Mercedes Moran and Ruth Zwick were fighting? Right before Mercedes bit the dust?"

Jon said, "The day she met the Grim Reaper."

Kevin rolled his eyes. I said, "Nearly everyone there was recording the fight with their cell phones. I mentioned it to you before, Kev."

"I know. UCLA PD sent out a request for people to send in their video, but no one responded."

"I bet a lot of those videos are posted now on YouTube or Facebook pages. What if you look at the backgrounds of the clips? See if there's anyone there that doesn't belong?"

Jon asked, "How would we know if someone didn't belong?"

Kevin said, "We wouldn't. But we could at least see if there was anyone there that we haven't talked to yet."

Hopkins whistled. "I admire your get up and go, Detective Brodie. We've run ourselves ragged going through these lists with a fine-toothed comb, talking to every Tom, Dick and Harriet at this conference, but you're ready to go to the ends of the earth to track down the perpetrator of this dastardly deed."

Kevin said, "*Somebody* stuck a sharp object into Mercedes Moran. I do *not* want this case to go cold."

Jon said, "We're not giving up the ship."

Hopkins beamed. "You two are the dynamic duo, all right. It ain't over 'til it's over. We've got to keep our eyes on the prize until it's mission accomplished."

Even Jon rolled his eyes that time. Kevin said weakly, "Yes, sir."

Liz and I were relieved at reference by Lola Mack and Isabel Gutierrez. The police headed for Café 451, and Liz and I went upstairs. I logged onto my computer and did a search for video of the fight. By the time Kevin, Jon and Hopkins arrived at my door, fresh cups of coffee in their hands, I'd found three distinct views of the altercation.

Hopkins said, "All right. Let's take a look see at these videos."

Two of the clips were from YouTube and one from Facebook, which I could see using Kristen's account. I turned my computer monitor in the opposite direction, toward the door, so all three cops didn't have to crowd behind my desk.

"Okay, here goes. This first one is very close to the angle that Kristen and I had on the fight." I clicked on the link.

On screen Ruth Zwick was yelling at Mercedes. Jon asked, "Do all of those faces look familiar to you, Kev?"

Kevin studied the crowd of about ten women who'd been standing to Mercedes's right, opposite me. "I think so. I know we've talked to her and her…" He pointed.

Jon said glumly, "No one stands out."

Hopkins said, "No worries, boys. This is a shot in the dark. If none of these ladies pans out, don't let it put a damper on your spirits."

Kevin said, "Right. Let's see the rest of this one."

We watched as Ruth attacked Mercedes. I heard the guy from the sci-fi aisle say, "Cool! Catfight." Then I showed up, pulling Ruth off Mercedes and telling them to cut it out.

Hopkins admired my work. "Timing is everything, Dr. Brodie. Lucky for us you were waiting in the wings."

We watched the video through to the end, where I asked the UCLA cops to escort Mercedes out and they left. I ran it again, stopping at a couple of places to let Jon and Kevin look at faces in the crowd. Kevin said, "We've spoken to all of them."

"Okay." I cued up the second video. "This one is taken from behind Ruth. You can see Mercedes straight on."

We watched it twice with the same result. No one appeared that Jon and Kevin didn't recognize. I said, "Okay, one more. This one was shot from the opposite angle, right across from Kristen and me."

The video played for a few seconds then Kevin said, "Freeze it there."

Kristen and I were in the frame this time. I recognized the "catfight" guy, the government thriller guy, a couple of other exhibitors, and… Hopkins said, "Oho. Lookie there. Our bad actor from the Sunshine State is impersonating a fly on the wall."

Guy Testaverde was standing behind the thriller author we'd spoken to, a smirk plastered across his face. I said, "I went through the exhibit hall this morning, and Guy has cleared out."

Kevin said, "Yeah. The Tequesta Internal Affairs guy arrested him yesterday."

Jon said, "He's cooling his heels in the Metro Center Jail until we clear him for Moran's murder. Or not."

Hopkins said, "And if not? Mr. Testaverde wins a one-way ticket to San Quentin."

Kevin and Jon studied the screen for another moment, then Jon pointed at it. "There's a new face in the crowd."

I looked closer. Standing just at the edge of the throng, to my left, was a vaguely familiar elderly lady. Kevin said, "Check out the expression on her face."

The old lady looked - intent. And inordinately pleased.

Hopkins said, "Whew. If looks could kill, eh? That's a Cheshire Cat smile if ever I saw one. But how will you get a handle on her identity?"

I said, "I've seen her before. She sat in my row during the keynote speech."

Jon frowned. "Are you sure it's the same woman?"

"Almost sure. I remember thinking she could be Norman Rockwell's idea of a grandmother. And she was wearing that sweater." The garment in question was kelly green in color. Memorable. I noticed the soft-sided bag dangling from her elbow and remembered… "That bag holds knitting supplies. She was knitting during the keynote. Could Mercedes have been stabbed with a knitting needle?"

Jon asked, "Are they sharp enough for that?"

"I don't know."

Kevin said, "Jamie, email me that link. We'll go to the conference and show it around. See if anyone recognizes her."

"Before you do that, let me try something." I took a screenshot of the paused video and manipulated it until the only whole face in the photo belonged to the old lady. Then I uploaded it to Google's image search. "Let's see if we can identify her this way."

Hopkins was impressed. "Well, well, *well*. What will they think of next? This old dog is learning some new tricks."

I wasn't expecting results. I considered telling my partners in crime that I only held out a glimmer of hope for identifying the old lady, but I suspected that Kevin might Tase me. I was shocked when a page full of images appeared that presented a selection of elderly ladies in single and group photos.

Hopkins squinted at the screen and pointed. "Is that our person of interest?"

Kevin said, "I think so. Jamie, do the pictures tell who she is?"

I clicked on the photo, which took me to the website of the First Baptist Church of Vermilion, Illinois. "Yep. Her name is Mavis Osterhout. Chair of the Altar Guild."

"Spell that." Kevin entered the name into his phone. He must have texted; a few seconds later the phone buzzed. "Tim says she's registered at the conference."

Jon said, "I'll start calling hotels." He left the office.

Hopkins said, "Good work, young man. Pardon my French, but you're a hell of an investigator yourself."

I said, "I've had a lot of practice."

As soon as I said it, I knew I'd walked right into it. From the look on Kevin's face, he knew it too. Hopkins grinned widely. "You know what they say. Practice makes perfect."

Kevin closed his eyes and shook his head. I said, "Yes, sir."

Chapter 25
Rank Has Its Privileges

In a few minutes, Jon was back. "Got it in one. I started with the closest hotel and that's where Mavis Osterhout is registered. I sent Elias and Jill to pick her up. They'll take her to our station."

Hopkins shook his head. "Hard to imagine that sweet old lady as a menace to society."

Jon said, "Anything is possible. She might have considered herself an avenging angel."

Hopkins nodded sagely. "Entirely possible that she had an axe to grind. Not to change horses in the middle of the stream, but inquiring minds want to know. How long have you fellas been with LAPD?"

Kevin said, "Fifteen years."

Jon said, "Thirteen for me."

"Think you'll retire from West LA Homicide?"

Kevin and Jon looked at each other. I knew they were wondering how much information to entrust to an IAG lieutenant. Jon said, "I haven't thought that far ahead." Which wasn't entirely true.

Hopkins said, "It's never too soon to plan for the future, you know. You boys play your cards right, I'll put a bug in the ear of the head honcho at Homicide Special. Do everything in my power to pull some strings for you. You'll be sitting pretty."

Kevin said, "I'm studying for a master's degree in social work. I'm hoping to join the Victim Impact Program with the DA's office."

Hopkins looked surprised. "Oho! Good for you. What about you, Detective Eckhoff? Think you might set your sights on a downtown gig?"

Jon said, "As in Homicide Special?"

I knew Jon had already made preliminary moves toward Homicide Special. He'd talked to Detective Simon, with whom he'd worked on the Stacks Strangler case, and had been networking in preparation for promotion to Detective III.

What I didn't know was how an IAG lieutenant could help him with that.

"That's what I'm talking about. You're exactly the brand of cowboy that rodeo likes to sign up. Relatively young, great solve rate, clean record, smart as a whip, ready and willing to put the long hours in. You're holding all the right cards."

When Hopkins had said "cowboy," Jon began to smile. "You think I'd be a good fit?"

Kevin said, "Of course you would."

Hopkins nodded sagely. "Your partner hit the bullseye. No ifs, ands or buts about it. Lord knows that department could use some fresh blood. You'd be just the ticket."

Jon said, "I've spoken with Detective Simon a couple of times already. He's given me some pointers."

Hopkins looked surprised. "How do you know Jermaine?"

So *that* was his first name. I'd always wondered. Jon said, "We worked together on the Stacks Strangler case."

"Ah, yes." Hopkins raised an eyebrow. "That was the case that put Carl Zurowski out to pasture."

Uh oh. Detective Zurowski, Simon's then-partner in Homicide Special, had been pulled from the Stacks Strangler case when I'd filed a complaint about his homophobic insults. I hoped Hopkins and Zurowski hadn't been buddies. Jon said, "I knew he'd been removed from the case, but I didn't know he'd been canned."

"The way I heard it, he threw a hissy fit in the squad room when the boss told him he was off the case and called Jermaine every name in the book. The boss had been looking for a reason to kick him to the curb, and Zurowski finally handed him one on a silver platter. Long overdue, if you ask me."

I was glad to hear that Hopkins hadn't been a Zurowski fan. Jon said, "I'd hate to think there are others like him in Homicide Special. Might not be a pleasant atmosphere."

Hopkins waved that off. "Oh, you don't have to worry about that. Most of the old guard has packed it in. The bosses are hoping to attract bright young things like yourself."

Jon's expression was unreadable - a first, in my experience. "Good to know."

Hopkins slapped his thighs and stood up. "Well, boys, I've got to get home to the little woman. See you fellas bright and early, eh?"

Kevin said, "Yes, sir."

We watched Hopkins leave. I said, "Do you think he's here to recruit for Homicide Special?"

Jon said, "That doesn't make sense. Why would they send an IAG guy for that?"

Kevin said, "He seems to be well-connected. I hope he's telling the truth about being able to help you with that."

"Yeah. Me too."

Kevin's phone rang, and he checked the caller ID. "Hey, Jill. No? Okay. No - she could be anywhere at that conference. Ask the front desk people to call you when she comes back in. You bet. Thanks."

I said, "Mavis is in the wind?"

Kevin gave me a sour look but said, "Yeah. She hasn't checked out of the hotel."

"So what happened in San Francisco? With Mercedes's former co-worker?"

"Ah." Jon dropped into one of my visitor chairs and propped his feet on my desk. "The guy - his name is Ian Hughes - remembered Tammy Thomas well."

Kevin sat in the other chair. "Hughes said that Tammy was always secretive. She was an outstanding programmer but not likable."

I said, "IT people are not always adept at social niceties."

Jon said, "True, but according to Hughes, Tammy was particularly - the word he used was *irascible*. He did say, though, that she was always bragging about a program she was writing on her own time that would make her rich. She never gave any hint as to what it was."

I said, "Might have been an app or a game that she intended to sell."

"Maybe." Kevin yawned. "Hughes said that their supervisor ran scans on Tammy's computer to make sure she wasn't working on her own program on the job. But she wasn't. We hope that whatever it was is still on the computers we confiscated."

"So what's your working theory now? Who killed Mercedes?"

Jon and Kevin sighed simultaneously, then chuckled about it. Jon said, "Our best guess? The killer was the next person on Moran's list to be outed."

Kevin said, "Kristen told me about her idea that Mercedes was going for publicity. Maybe she did have an even more shocking announcement to make at the keynote and Martie Pepper interrupted her."

I said, "She had the attention of the self-publishing world at that moment. If she had something else up her sleeve, she must have been planning to spill the beans right then and there."

Jon grinned. "Maybe she was too smart for her own good."

Kevin grunted his annoyance. "I suspect that this woman at the Library of Congress will be involved somehow."

"She hasn't called you back yet?"

"Nope."

Jon slapped his knees and stood. "When she does? You'll be the first to know."

Kevin's phone rang as he stood up. I said, "Is that her?"

Jon said, "Is Mavis back already?"

"No, this is Sergeant Pope." Kevin answered, "Brodie. Yes, Sergeant. Oh, fantastic. What did she have to say?" He listened for a moment, a smile spreading across his face. "No kidding. No, if you're satisfied that she's truthful, that's good enough for me. Yep, we'll handle it. Thanks, Sergeant." He ended the call, grinning. "The woman who took you to see Moran's body showed up at UCLA PD a while ago."

I applauded. "*Yes*. What did she have to say for herself?"

"That she'd discovered the body when she went behind the curtain in search of folding chairs for a friend's booth. She latched onto you because she'd seen you break up the fight between Moran and Ruth Zwick and you were the first person she spotted that might be an authority figure. She ran off because you scared her."

Huh? "I *scared* her? How?"

"She told Pope that as soon as you saw Moran you said, 'Jesus fucking Christ on a cracker, not again.' It was the *not again* part that made her nervous. She started to wonder if you were involved somehow."

I rolled my eyes. "For God's sake. Does Pope want you to march me down there so he can throw the book at me? Take the rubber hose to me?"

Kevin said, "Nah. He's leaving your fate in our hands."

I snorted. "I *hope* he realizes he'd be wasting his breath."

Jon said, "Poor lady. She thought you might be hazardous to her health."

I grinned. "She did come across as a nervous Nellie."

He laughed. "Guess you had to be there."

Kevin groaned. "Oh, my *God*. Will you two *stop* it?"

Jon elbowed him. "Nip it in the bud, in other words? Never fear, pardner. This too shall pass. Let's go back to the shop and see what we can find out about Mavis Osterhout."

I said, "Keep me in the loop?"

Kevin sighed. "You have Date Night tonight, right?"

"Yeah." We were keeping it simple - dinner at the Indian restaurant around the corner from our house. "You can text me, though."

Jon said, "Ending the week on a high note, huh?"

"Yep. Tonight we'll be footloose and fancy free."

Kevin growled and dragged Jon out of my office.

Chapter 26
Ancient History

When I got home, I found a box from Loving Men Publishing inside the gate where UPS had left it. My romance books had arrived as I'd hoped, just in time for the weekend. I carried the box to the office where Pete was at his laptop. "Hey, our books came."

"Huh." He watched as I opened the box. "Let me see."

I handed him the books, and he frowned at the cover. "Where are their heads?"

I laughed. "In your imagination."

He radiated skepticism. I didn't blame him.

I changed into jeans, and Pete and I set out on foot to the restaurant. After we ordered, Pete said, "There's something I should probably tell you before Aaron comes tomorrow afternoon."

Uh oh. "What?"

"Back before Aaron met Paul, while you were dating Eric - Aaron and I considered dating each other."

"Oh." That was a relief; I'd been afraid that Pete was going to tell me that he and Aaron had slept together. "Why didn't you?"

"We'd both just been hired at SMC. Neither of us thought it was a good idea to be involved with a coworker."

I shrugged. "You'd probably have done well together."

Pete looked surprised. "You think?"

"Yeah. You're a lot alike, you're close friends - it might have worked."

"You're not jealous."

"No. I mean, I'm glad you never slept with him - you never slept with him, did you?"

Pete laughed. "No."

"But given that, no. I'm not jealous. I like Aaron a lot, he's an attractive guy, and you've been friends for a long time. I can see why you would have considered it."

"I can't believe Paul has screwed him over like this." Pete scowled. "Every time I think about it, it makes me angry."

"Me, too. Did Aaron know who Paul had been with?"

"Some real estate agent. Aaron never met the guy."

I wrinkled my nose. "I guess Paul has plenty of opportunity to meet real estate agents in empty houses."

"Yeah. Bastard."

Chapter 27
Every Dog Has His Day

We lingered over dinner and strolled home, stopping to chat with our neighbor, Helen Quintero, who was in her front-yard garden. It was nearly dark when we opened our front door - and stopped stock still just inside.

Our living room floor was littered with a blizzard of shredded yellow paper. Ammo was sitting in the center of it, his tail swishing bits of paper from side to side. His ears were perked and he was panting happily - but he hadn't met us at the door. He knew he'd done something wrong.

Pete and I said in unison, "*Ammo. What the hell!*"

He scrambled to his feet and trotted to us, his ears and head lowered but his tail still wagging. He'd heard the tone of our voices and was begging forgiveness. I said, "Ammo. What did you *do?*"

Pete picked up a bit of the paper. "What is this?"

I scooped up a handful of confetti and examined it. "It's the Yellow Pages."

"Holy shit. Did he shred the whole *book?*"

Once a year, we received a print copy of the Los Angeles area Yellow Pages. We never requested it; the book simply appeared. It was massive, a brick of paper that we'd never consulted. It always sat in the same spot, on one side of the bottom shelf of our TV stand in the living room. Ammo had never demonstrated any interest in it in the nearly two years we'd had him.

I located a larger section of heavier paper that had comprised part of a cover and showed it to Pete. "I believe so."

Pete rested his hands on his hips. "Ammo. Why did you do this?"

Ammo wagged his tail faster. I said, "He's bored."

"How can he be bored? I'm home with him all day."

"Yeah, but you're not *interacting* with him all day. He got spoiled over the summer when he was getting lots of attention from Dad while we were overseas, then from us while we were in New Mexico. We're back in our routine of working all day and he doesn't like it."

Pete sighed, shaking his head at Ammo. "What are we gonna do with you, buddy?"

I could swear that Ammo was grinning. I said, "I'll get the broom."

Chapter 28
Kids, Don't Try This At Home

Once I'd cleaned up the mess, we took Ammo for a walk and promised him a trip to the dog park in the morning. When we got home, it was time for bed. When I came out of the bathroom after brushing my teeth, Pete was sitting in bed, his back against the headboard. He'd stacked the gay romance books on his bedside table and he picked the top one from the stack and showed me the cover. "Want to try this one? It's about law enforcement."

"Sure." I climbed into bed and read the title. "*Colton's Promise*. Colton, huh?"

Pete grinned. "According to the blurb, Colton is an FBI Special Agent. The other guy, Chase, is NCIS."

"Ooh. Mortal enemies. Allow me to make a prediction." I counted on my fingers. "One. Chase of NCIS has a case, and Special Agent Colton elbows in on it. It's hate at first sight. Two. Chase and Colton are forced to work together by their respective supervisors. Three. In spite of their mutual hatred, Chase and Colton are incredibly attracted to each other. They fight it but end up having steamy sex. Four. Mutual hatred resumes after steamy sex and each attempts to convince himself that it was *only* sex. Five. Eventually they're forced to trust each other, or one of them has to save the other's life, and they realize they're soulmates."

"I thought you'd never read any of these before."

"I haven't. I might be entirely wrong. But one summer when we were in South Carolina I was resting after an asthma attack, got bored, and raided a box of books that apparently had belonged to my grandmother. There were dozens of Harlequin romances. The plot lines were always *quite* similar... except the steamy sex didn't happen until they were married." I tapped the cover of the book. "Guys won't wait that long to have steamy sex."

"How does your fourth plot point fit your grandmother's stash?"

"In Regency times, marriages were arranged for political or financial gain. Usually the couple still hated each other once they were married."

Pete chuckled. "Shall we see if you're right?"

"Sure."

He opened the book, and we read the first few pages. The plot hinged on the kidnapping of a naval officer's six-year-old daughter. Pete said, "Okay. I can see where NCIS and FBI *might* both be involved in this."

"Don't expect the investigation to conform exactly to standard procedure."

He smirked. "It's already superior to Guy Testaverde's interpretation, though."

"*That's* a low bar."

We read on, Pete occasionally muttering at some phrase that would never be uttered by a cop in real life. The first steamy sex scene occurred in chapter two. I hadn't been sure what to expect - but I *had* been expecting action that was anatomically possible. Pete stopped, frowning. "Wait a minute. Chase is fucking Colton *and* sucking him off at the *same time??*"

I said, "Chase missed his calling. He should be with Cirque du Soleil."

"That's too implausible to be arousing."

He was right. My attempt to work out the mechanics had stripped any scrap of sensuality from the scene. I said, "This was written by a woman and mostly will be read by women. Do you suppose *they* believe that scene is possible?"

Pete shook his head. "I think that bothers me more than the law enforcement inaccuracies."

"Why?"

"When average straight people learn you're gay, where's the first place their minds go? They picture us having sex."

"Yeah." I'd read that reaction in more than one facial expression over the years.

He jabbed a finger at the page bearing the sex scene. "This can only contribute to that. If a straight woman has read this, or anything similar, and believes this is the kind of sex we have - no *wonder* they think we're all kinky and horny."

"Maybe the next sex scene will be better."

But it wasn't. Two chapters later, Chase was straddling a bathroom sink, facing Colton, as Colton fucked him. I said, "Um -"

Pete was laughing. "Okay, first. What bathroom sink would support a guy who's been described as 220 pounds of chiseled steel?"

"Second, where are Chase's balls, and why aren't they impeding Colton's access? And third - just how well-endowed is Colton, that his dick reaches that far?"

Pete tossed the book onto the bedside table. "Now *that* sounds like it was originally written for a het couple. Remove the woman and replace her with 220 pounds of chiseled steel."

I poked him in the ribs. "I bet you could write these. Your plots would have to be similar, but you'd at least get the law enforcement terminology right and your sex scenes would be physically possible."

"Nah. You said these books were the publisher's bestsellers, right? Clearly the readers want -" He jerked his thumb at the nightstand. "- *that*."

"I guess." I whacked my pillow into shape and scooted down into bed.

Pete did the same. "So your grandmother was a romance fan, huh?"

"It seems so. I asked Sarge about it after I found those books. He said something like, 'Your gramma had some nutty ideas.' We left it at that. The next day, he carried the box to the public library's donation bin. I guess reading romance is an escape from the daily drag of real life, huh?"

"Sure. It allows women to fantasize about being taken care of instead of them having to take care of everyone else. Think about your grandmother. Every day - Sarge's uniforms have to be clean and pressed, Sarge and the kids have to be fed. With three boys, there'd be tons of laundry. And she had a huge garden, right?"

"Yeah. And I'm confident that Sarge wasn't the most romantic of husbands. She deserved her escapism."

Pete rolled up on his side, propping his head on his hand. He was grinning. "I guess our romance wouldn't make the bestseller lists."

I grinned back. "We liked each other from the beginning, and two *years* passed before the first sex scene. Who wants to read about *that?*"

Saturday, September 30

Chapter 29
Seek and Ye Shall Find

We'd intended to go for a run the next morning, but when Pete came back inside with the newspaper, he was shaking his head. "It's too smoggy for you to be outside. It's too smoggy for *me* to be outside."

"Oh. Crap. What about the dog park?"

"Nope." Pete tossed the newspaper in my direction. "I'm gonna take a shower."

I checked email while I waited my turn and found a message from my editor at Oxford University Press, David Beaton.

Hello Jamie

I've taken one last pass through the manuscript and made a few more notes. Please read and we'll discuss.

Cheers

David

I opened the manuscript and waited for it to load, re-reading the first page - the acknowledgements page - as it did.

Thanks to the following librarians: Niles Gretton, Merton College, Oxford; Fiona Mackenzie, University of Edinburgh; Moira Fraser, Forres Library...

I stopped as it hit me.

Acknowledgements.

Every author had an acknowledgements page. Surely, Mercedes Moran was no exception.

I picked up my phone, opened the Kindle app, and downloaded Mercedes's first five and last five books, hoping I didn't have to waste any more than ten dollars on this quest.

Pete came into the office, wearing jeans but shirtless, rubbing his hair dry. "Whatcha doing?"

"I had an idea. Another place where Mercedes Moran might have mentioned people's names. In her acknowledgements." I pointed to the screen of my phone, which was displaying my Kindle library. "I just downloaded ten of her books."

He winced. "Damn, I hate to send any money her way. Even if it is only to her estate."

"Hey, maybe Martie Pepper will end up with the bulk of Mercedes's estate. Anyway, I had to check this. The conference ends tomorrow. Kev and Jon are running out of time."

He shrugged. "Okay. Your turn in the shower."

"In a sec. Just let me check one." I turned back to my phone and opened the first book. *Violets Are Forever.* Fortunately there was a linked table of contents, which allowed me to click right through to the Acknowledgements.

There was only one name.

Thanks to Almanzo Norwich. Couldn't have done it without you.

I checked the rest of the books. They were all the same. Almanzo Norwich, whoever he was, was the star of Mercedes's show.

I called Kevin. When he answered, I said, "Hey. I have another name for you." I told him what I'd discovered.

"Almanzo Norwich? He's in every book?"

"Yup."

"Huh. Hang on." He lowered the phone, and I heard him ask Jon, "What did IT say?"

In the background Jon said, "They haven't cracked the password yet."

"Tell 'em to try the name Almanzo Norwich."

Jon said, "*What?*"

Kevin spelled it. "Mercedes thanked him, whoever he is, in her books. Jamie found the name."

"Okay."

I heard Jon speak to someone else and Kevin returned to our conversation. I asked, "Have you found Mavis Osterhout?"

"According to her hotel, she hasn't checked out yet. The concierge told us she was on a bus tour of the stars' homes."

I laughed. "God bless the tourists."

"Yeah, right. We did find her address and phone number in Illinois, but there's no other information online. When we called, no one answered."

"Maybe she lives alone."

"Possible." He sighed. "I don't know that she's even…"

My phone beeped with a text. I glanced at the screen and said, "Hey, Kristen just texted me."

"Okay. Thanks for the tip."

"Want me to see what I can find on the web about Norwich?"

"Sure. Thanks."

I said goodbye to Kevin and read my text from Kristen. *What are you doing this morning?*

Was going to the dog park, but it's too smoggy. What's up?

I have an idea about Mercedes. Could use your help.

Cool. Want me to come over?

I'll come there. See you in 30.

Chapter 30
A Good Man is Hard to Find

I took my shower and dressed. Kristen appeared at the back door 32 minutes later, laptop case slung over her shoulder. Pete let her in. "Want a Coke?"

"Please. And your wireless password."

Kristen and I sat on the sofa, drinks at hand, and logged on. I said, "What's your idea?"

"Instagram." She opened the site. "I searched Mercedes's account, but she only posted pictures of cover reveals. Then it occurred to me this morning that I hadn't searched for her on other people's accounts. If I can find photos of her with other people, we can do your trick with the images search and identify them."

"Okay. I'm going to see what I can find on this Almanzo Norwich guy, too."

Kristen looked puzzled. "Who's that?"

I explained. She said, "Almanzo, huh? Whoever he is, his mother must have been a *Little House on the Prairie* fan."

"Why?"

"That's the only other place I've ever heard the name Almanzo. Laura Ingalls grew up and married Almanzo Wilder." She tapped my screen. "You'd better check all of her other books for names, too."

"I'm going to. As soon as I find out who Norwich is."

We went to work. I immediately discovered that Almanzo Norwich didn't seem to exist. A Google search for the name produced only two results on Google, both in French, and both apparently about soccer teams.

Beside me, Kristen was sifting through photos. I turned to UCLA's newspaper databases and searched for Norwich there. Nothing. I expanded the search to all of our databases. Same lack of results. I searched Melvyl, the union catalog for the entire University of California system; WorldCat, a catalog from libraries worldwide; and the Library of Congress. Nothing. I went back to the internet and used every non-Google search engine I could think of. Nada. I even combed the FamilySearch genealogy website. Zip.

I texted Kevin. *Almanzo Norwich doesn't seem to exist, unless you guys can locate him in your databases. I've looked everywhere.*

He responded, *So have we. Didn't find anything. BUT his name and a date opened both of Moran's computers.*

No kidding! What date?

Funny you should ask. Stella Kim emailed me court documents on Tammy Thomas's name change last night. Date was the exact day that Mercedes Moran came into being.

WHOA. What does THAT mean?

No idea yet. We're meeting with IT in 5 minutes to root through the drives. Is Kristen there?

Y.

She staying for lunch?

I said, "Kevin wants to know if you're staying for lunch."

She grinned. "If you'll feed me, sure."

Yes. You and Jon wanna come by?

Sure. See you at noon.

K.

I told Kristen about my fruitless quest. "How are you doing?"

"I've only found one so far." She pointed to the photo on her screen. "What does this look like to you?"

The picture was of a group of about eight people. Two were young men, one was a young woman, two were young people of indeterminate gender, two of them appeared to be drag queens, and one of them was Mercedes. Most of them were holding drinks. There was a disco ball in the background. I said, "Looks like a club. Where is that?"

"The other hashtag, besides Mercedes's name, is San Francisco."

"Who are those other people?"

"The Instagram account belongs to a Shannon Graves. He, she, or they could be any of these other people."

"Did he, she, or they tag anyone?"

"Only by username. Let me see if I can identify any of them." She began to click on names and scan photos.

I didn't hold out much hope that Kristen's discovery would lead anywhere. I went back to my Kindle app and reluctantly downloaded the rest of Mercedes's books, then began searching through acknowledgements pages.

I'd made it through the first twenty books - no one's name appeared other than Almanzo Norwich's - when Kristen said, "*Bingo!*"

"What?"

"This one." She pointed to one of the young guys in the original photo. "His screen name is FarmFreshinFrisco. Here's his photo stream." She switched tabs on the browser. "See anyone you recognize there?"

FarmFreshinFrisco was standing in what appeared to be an apartment, with his arm around Mavis Osterhout. Below the photo there was one hashtag.

#Grandma

I said, "I'll be *damned*. What's his name?"

"He doesn't provide it." Kristen took a screenshot of the page and pasted it into a text to Kevin and Jon. "Let me do an images search for him…" She performed the same maneuver that I'd used to locate Mavis.

"Anything?"

Kristen shook her head. "There are a few photos of him that are similar to one in the club, but none of them give his name."

Pete came downstairs from the office and asked, "You two getting anywhere?"

"Maybe." I gave him a synopsis. "Oh, and Kevin and Jon are coming by for lunch. In 45 minutes."

Pete laughed. "In that case, we're having BLTs."

He set to frying bacon while I searched through the rest of Mercedes's acknowledgements pages. After another twenty books, Almanzo Norwich was still her only apparent friend. I said to Kristen, "She didn't have an editor? She didn't have a cover artist? She didn't belong to a writing group?"

"Maybe she did all that herself."

I glanced over at her screen; she was on Amazon's website. I said, "What are you doing?"

"Looking at romance bestseller lists."

"Why?"

"I'm trying to make connections." She held up a finger. "We know Mercedes plagiarized from Angelica Ashley. We know that Mercedes was cranking out a book per month. We know - from the woman in front of us at the keynote speech - that she used nearly the same outline for every book." Kristen clicked on another tab and pointed at her screen. "This is Angelica Ashley's website, which someone seems to be maintaining."

I said, "Probably Martie."

"Right. Anyway, *Rose, Rise* was the number one bestseller in romance in December 2009. Six months later, Mercedes published her first book."

"*Violets Are Forever.*"

"Right. *Rose* stayed at the number one spot for a year. Martie Pepper said that Mercedes's first five books were plagiarized from *Rose.*"

I checked the titles in my Kindle library. "After *Violets*, Mercedes's second book was *Daisy in Chains.*"

From the kitchen, Pete started to laugh. "Kinky!"

Kristen grinned. "What were the titles of 3, 4, and 5?"

I read them off. "*By Any Other Name, Forget Me Not*, and *Ginn Blossoms.*"

"All flower-related. Then what was the title of the sixth book?"

"Um - *The Sacred Gate*. What took over the #1 spot from *Rose?*"

Kristen clicked on another tab. "*The Door of Secrets* by Celeste Estrada. Gate? Door? Coincidence?"

As soon as she'd spoken, someone started knocking on our back door. I laughed. "I think not!"

Chapter 31
Fact Is Stranger Than Fiction

Jon and Kevin were in their weekend working clothes - jeans, polos, and running shoes. Pete assembled and distributed BLTs, and Kristen and I told Jon and Kevin what we'd found. They scrutinized the photo of Mavis Osterhout with FarmFreshinFrisco.

Kevin said, "Okay, let me think out loud. This guy, who seems to be Mavis's grandson, is acquainted with Mercedes. But as far as we know, there's no other connection between Mavis and Mercedes. Mavis isn't an author, unless she's using a pen name that we haven't uncovered."

Jon said, "Then we have your theory about ongoing plagiarism on Mercedes's part. How would that work?"

Kristen retrieved a bit of bacon that had escaped from her sandwich and popped it into her mouth. "Suppose Mercedes did use the same outline for every book. She'd want to keep up with the trends in popular romance, right? That would increase her own chances of producing a bestseller. So she took names and characterization, maybe plot points, from other books, and plugged them into her outline."

I said, "To turn out a book a *month*, though? Even with names and plot points, that's awfully fast work."

Kevin said, "And there's no apparent connection…" He stopped as his phone rang. "Brodie. Hey, Mike. Yeah? What does it do?" He listened for a minute, his expression growing more astounded with each second. "You are *shitting* me. That explains a *lot*. Okay, thanks, dude. I owe you." He laughed. "Yeah, yeah." He said goodbye.

Jon said, "That was Mike in IT?"

"Yup. He found Almanzo Norwich. It's a computer program."

Kristen, Pete and I responded in unison. "A *computer* program??"

"Yes. Almanzo Norwich comes from A Matrix for Automatic Narrative Writing… I forget the rest. Anyway. Mercedes could write a book a month because she wasn't writing them. The computer program was. Mike found all of her files and confirmed it."

Jon said, "I bet that's what Mercedes - Tammy Thomas - bragged about to her coworker Ian Hughes. A program that was going to make her rich."

Pete finished his first sandwich and tackled his second. "But how would that result in her murder?"

Kevin shook his head. "I don't know. If someone found out..." He stopped as his phone rang again. "Oho. This is a DC area code. Quiet, everyone."

We fell silent. The caller must be the woman who worked for the copyright office. Kevin answered, "Los Angeles Police Department, Detective Brodie." He put the phone on speaker and laid it on the ottoman. "Ms. Forsythe, we're investigating the murder of an author named Mercedes Moran. We found your name in her phone contacts."

A querulous, high-pitched voice responded, "So what?"

Not exactly thrilled at the prospect of police interaction, then. Pete bit his lip to keep from laughing. Kevin said, "You're not in any trouble from us, Ms. Forsythe, but we need to know what transpired between you and Ms. Moran."

"I don't see what that has to do with her death."

Kevin gambled. "Ms. Forsythe, I seriously doubt that the copyright office would approve of your practice of releasing private information to third parties. You *will* be in deep trouble from us if you don't start answering my questions."

The voice got huffy. "Well, you seem to already know all about it."

I thought, *Aha.* Kevin said, "So you were supplying Mercedes Moran with the real names of other authors."

"Yes. She didn't tell me why she wanted them, and I didn't ask."

"Was she paying you for that?"

A pause and a sniff, then, "Yes. Five hundred dollars per name. Do you know how long it's been since I last had a raise?"

"Ms. Forsythe, we need the list of names."

"Can't you get that from her blog?"

"So you *do* know how Ms. Moran was using the names."

The woman's breath caught. She'd slipped up. "Well, I..."

Kevin said, "Ms. Forsythe. As I said, if you're cooperative, we'll have no reason to report your actions to your supervisors. When was the last time you supplied Ms. Moran with a name?"

"It was Monday."

"This past Monday?"

"Yes."

"Whose name was that?"

"Er - I'd have to consult my list."

Kevin was beginning to lose patience. "Well, then, please consult it."

"It's on a USB drive. I have to start my laptop."

"I'll wait."

The woman sighed. "*Fine*." It sounded like she'd set her phone aside. There was a pause, then the dulcet tones of Windows opening. Some typing and clicking occurred. A full minute later she picked the phone back up. "All right. There were two names last Monday. The first one was Dan Ross."

Dan Ross. I sucked in a breath, and Kevin shot me a warning look. Dan Ross - or another person of the same name - was the thriller writer we'd spoken to in the exhibit hall.

He'd been standing next to Guy Testaverde in the video of Mercedes's fight with Ruth Zwick.

Kevin said, "What was Mr. Ross's pen name?"

"Celeste Estrada."

Kristen and I stared at each other. Celeste Estrada was the author of *The Door of Secrets*, published right before Mercedes's book, *The Sacred Gate*.

Not to mention, another man writing as a woman. Kristen and I both turned to our laptops. She searched Amazon, and I went to Google.

Kevin was asking Muriel Forsythe, "What was the second name you gave to Ms. Moran on Monday?"

"Brenda Clancy."

"And what is her pen name?"

"Jared Henry."

Pete, Kristen and I looked at each other, startled. A woman using a man's name? We hadn't encountered *that* variation yet. Kevin said, "All right, thank you. What was the name before that?"

"Elmer Thrash." Ms. Forsythe sounded smug. "I made her pay extra for *that* one. Do you know *who* Elmer Thrash pretended to be?"

Kevin came across as bored. "Yes, ma'am, Angelica Ashley. What was the name before that?"

"Edna Brown. Pen name Carmen Hidalgo."

"Before that?"

"Ruth Zwick. Pen name Bethany May."

It sounded as if Mercedes had outed authors in the order in which Ms. Forsythe provided the names. Kevin said, "All right. Dan Ross and Brenda Clancy were the last names you provided to Ms. Moran?"

"Yes."

"Thank you. I need you to email me a copy of your list."

"What? *Why?*"

Kevin didn't bother to hide his irritation. "It's evidence in a homicide investigation, ma'am. You can come out here to testify if you'd rather."

"Fine! Fine! Give me your email address."

Kevin repeated his address. "Are you sending it right now?"

"Yes." I heard more clicking. "There. It should be on its way."

Kevin's phone dinged and he checked it quickly. "Yes, ma'am, there it is. We appreciate your cooperation."

"Whatever." Ms. Forsythe hung up. I thought about my cousin-in-law Blair and wondered if the entire Library of Congress was staffed by testy people.

Kristen was checking the master list of names she'd created. "Neither Brenda Clancy nor Jared Henry appear in any of Mercedes's online activity, nor is she registered at the conference. I don't have Dan Ross or Celeste Estrada on Mercedes's list either, but Dan Ross is registered at the conference."

Jon said, "Yeah. We talked to him the other day. I think we'd better talk to him again."

Kevin placed a call. "Hey, Jill. Two things. First, a guy registered at the conference named Dan Ross. Find him if you can and bring him in for an interview. Second, background on a woman named Brenda Clancy. Awesome, thanks. We'll be back at the station in about twenty minutes. See ya." He hung up.

Jon said, "Come on, pardner. We've got other fish to fry."

Kevin groaned. "One day. All I wanted was *one day* without a cliché."

Kristen snickered. Pete asked, "Where's Hopkins?"

Jon said, "He told us his plate was full today and he'd catch us on the rebound tomorrow."

Kevin said, "If there is a God, we'll make an arrest by tonight. There won't *be* a tomorrow with Hopkins."

I said, "You'd better get busy finding these people, then. Go cut 'em off at the pass."

Jon jumped to his feet. "We're in hot pursuit! Stay tuned!"

Kevin dragged Jon up the stairs and out the back door to the sound of our laughter.

Chapter 32
Like Something Out of a Novel

Kristen and I carried dirty plates to the kitchen. Pete started prepping for our dinner with Aaron as Kristen and I resumed the hunt.

I said, "Who do you want? Dan Ross and Celeste Estrada or Jared Henry and Brenda Clancy?"

"I'll take Jared and Brenda."

"Okay."

Googling Dan Ross led me to his website, where he promoted his government thrillers - and revealed that he was a former FBI agent. A former FBI agent, writing romance novels under a woman's name.

I said out loud, "Stranger things have happened."

Kristen said, "What?"

"Dan Ross is former FBI."

"Hm." She turned back to her screen.

Googling Dan's alter ego, Celeste Estrada, led me to *her* website, where she promoted her romance novels. She had a Twitter account but no Facebook page. There were no candid photos of Celeste anywhere that I could find. When I searched Google Images for her cover photo, it led me to a stock photo site.

I found that two of Celeste's books were in Amazon's top 100 romance bestsellers. She had fourteen novels to her name, and all of them had been top 10 bestsellers in romance e-books. Like Mercedes Moran, she didn't seem to publish in print.

I reported my findings to Kristen. "Nothing jumps out as problematic so far, other than Celeste being in direct competition with Mercedes."

"Unless Dan Ross was desperate to hide Celeste's true identity for some reason. If he's *former* FBI, why would he care about that?"

"Dunno. Kev and Jon will have to ask him. Have you uncovered anything?"

Kristen sighed. "The only links to Jared Henry that I get from Google are to his social media sites and to Amazon et al. Brenda Clancy doesn't exist online at *all*."

"Is it known that Jared Henry is a woman?"

"Not that I can see." Kristen waved her hand at her screen. "Google has failed me. I need to branch out."

"Have you tried metasearch?"

"Yeah. Nothing." Kristen paused as her phone dinged with a text. "Oo, oo, oo. Jill ran background on Brenda Clancy. She and Mavis Osterhout live in the same town, and Brenda Clancy's maiden name was Osterhout."

"*Whoa.* Is Brenda Mavis's *daughter?*"

"Has to be *some* kind of relative." Kristen read on. "Brenda is 47. That's the right age to be Mavis's daughter… She and her husband own a dairy farm and a general store in Vermillion, Illinois. Jill called their landline and no one answered."

"They're probably out milking the cows." I tapped my computer screen. "Let's approach this logically, assuming that Brenda is Mavis's daughter. Is there a reason that Brenda and Mavis would want to hide the fact that Brenda is Jared Henry? Other than possibly affecting sales?"

"Or simply that it's nobody else's business?"

"But is that worth *killing* for?"

Kristen spread her hand. "Is twenty bucks worth killing for? But it happens."

"What genre does Jared Henry write?"

"Mystery. Police procedural in a fictional Midwestern university town."

"That sounds benign enough. Why would that cause Brenda to hide Jared's identity at all costs?"

"I don't know. Let me check Amazon." Kristen typed, gnawing her lower lip. "Okay - here's his latest book. We can read the first chapter for free."

I leaned in to see Kristen's screen. The first chapter introduced the crime and the detectives; there didn't seem to be anything remotely controversial. I said, "Let's see the reviews."

The average of the reviews was around four stars, with an even division between three-, four-, and five-star reviews. With one exception. I pointed. "Click on that."

The one-star review was brief.

A friend recommended this author. Be advised - the main character is GAY. The author should state that in the blurb so that decent, God-fearing readers aren't caught unawares by this deviance.

Kristen grunted. "Lovely."

I said, "Oooookay. Brenda lives in a small town in Illinois. She's a dairy farmer. Rural Illinois is likely to be conservative. Brenda and her family are probably known in the community. They probably attend church. They probably depend on the community to buy their dairy products and shop at their store. For whatever reason, Brenda decides to write a gay character, but she knows her neighbors and church people would find that *deviant*. So she can't afford for anyone to uncover her writing identity."

Kristen nodded slowly. "Makes sense. Let's also speculate that Mavis is Brenda's mom. Maybe Mavis is unlike her peers and cool with Brenda's sideline. And, like many moms, Mavis is a mama bear who will defend her child at any cost."

"Okay, but there's one major problem. How would Mavis and Brenda have found out that Mercedes was planning to expose Brenda? For that matter, how would Dan Ross have learned that Mercedes was about to out him as Celeste Estrada? From what you and I have found, Mercedes doesn't even hint at who she's about to expose until she does it."

"Right. So we're missing a piece. Maybe the woman at the copyright office told someone else about her connection with Mercedes and that person passed on the information? But that seems unlikely."

I agreed. "We know there's a human link between Mercedes and Mavis - that kid in the photo that called Mavis grandma. Maybe he's Brenda's son. Maybe Mercedes confided in or bragged to him about what she was doing and named names. Maybe he passed on the information."

"Could be. That doesn't explain Dan Ross, though."

"No…"

Kristen's phone rang with the opening bars of the theme song from *Dragnet*. Kevin. She answered, "Hey. Have you found Dan or Mavis yet? Oh, good grief. Did the hotel not call you? Oh. Yeah, we're thinking that maybe Mavis is Brenda's mom, and Brenda is mom to the kid in the picture with Mercedes. Brenda's books are gay mysteries. That might not go over well among the good people of

Vermillion, Illinois." She snickered. "Okay. Yeah, I'm going home soon. See ya later. Love you, too."

She hung up. "Mavis returned from her tour of the stars' homes and jumped right on another bus for an excursion to Knott's Berry Farm. Dan Ross is still registered at his hotel but not in his room. Patrol officers are staking out both rooms."

I logged out of my laptop. "I vote that we let Kev and Jon figure the rest of this out. Mavis and Dan can't hide from them for too much longer."

Pete leaned toward the door, his hand cupped behind his ear. I said, "What?"

He grinned. "I thought I heard a fat lady singing…"

Chapter 33
A Sadder but Wiser Man

Once Kristen left, Pete and I hustled to get the rest of our chores done, not knowing exactly when Aaron would arrive - but we needn't have. The doorbell didn't ring until 5:30.

I opened the front door to see Aaron standing forlornly at the gate. He smiled when he saw me, but it didn't reach his eyes. I unlocked the gate as Ammo scampered up behind me.

Aaron's smile widened, and he bent down to ruffle Ammo's ears. "Hey, Ammo. Good boy."

I locked the gate behind Aaron. "Come on in."

"Thanks." He trailed me into the house.

I said, "So the USC gig is going well?"

"It is. I thought I'd miss teaching, but I don't."

Pete came down from the kitchen and gave Aaron a backslapping hug. "Just in time. Does mahi mahi sound good?"

"You bet."

I'd promised to cook so that Pete and Aaron could talk. Pete loaded three plates with his homemade coleslaw and fried green tomatoes while I broiled the filets. He asked Aaron, "Have you and Paul talked yet?"

"Not much. He has apologized and agreed to counseling. You and Jamie saw Tania Bibbins, right?"

"Right. She was terrific for us."

"I'm gonna call her Monday." Aaron's tone was dispirited. "I guess I should have expected it. He cheated *with* me. It's not a stretch to imagine that he'd cheat *on* me. But we're *married*. I guess I thought that would change things. Pretty stupid, huh?"

"No, no, *no*." Pete was emphatic. "You were *not* stupid. Marriage may not have prevented Paul from wanting to see other guys, but it *should* have made him discuss it with you first."

"I expect he was afraid I'd say no."

I turned the fish. Aaron was probably right about that. But discussing whether your relationship would be open or closed was practically Marriage 101. Pete and I had done it well before we were married.

Pete asked, "*Would* you have said no?"

"Before this happened, I thought of myself as open minded enough to consider it. But my reaction to this indicates - to me, at least - that my expectation was monogamy."

"Maybe your expectation was *honesty*."

Aaron barked a laugh. "Yeah. It was."

"Which is more than reasonable."

Aaron sighed. "I'd even considered bringing it up. We've been together six years. Our sex life was becoming predictable, and neither of us was thrilled with that. But - I never dreamed he'd go ahead and act without discussing it first."

I tested the fish. It was done, so I slid the filets onto a plate. "Dinner is served, gentlemen."

"Good." Aaron picked up his fork. "Let's change the subject while we eat."

We - more accurately, Pete and Aaron - talked about the paper they'd be collaborating on. I listened, knowing I'd be gathering research for the literature review. Aaron mentioned some of the specifics of the study, which led to a more general discussion of his and Pete's new jobs. Aaron asked, "Do you believe that teaching online will satisfy you long term?"

"I doubt it. But it's fine for now, and I start a part-time counseling gig next week." He told Aaron the details. "Have you talked to Curtis or Elliott recently?"

Curtis Glover was the remaining member of the psychology faculty at Santa Monica College, the only full-time instructor who'd stayed on after the scandal. Aaron said, "Paul and I had dinner with Elliott and Stewart about a week before - before I saw Paul's phone. Elliott said things were working out. Audra's teaching two online classes as an adjunct, and they hired two full-time people right out of Ph.D. programs who are young and enthusiastic. Elliott and Verlene have both decided to stay for now." Audra Rock was another of Aaron and Pete's colleagues who had left the college; Verlene Canaday was the chair of the psychology department.

Pete raised an eyebrow. "They only replaced two full-timers?"

"So far. Elliott's teaching three classes, Verlene's teaching one, and Curtis has an overload. They're searching for a third person but haven't found the right fit yet."

I said, "Cutting the budget through attrition. Sounds familiar."

Aaron nodded. "I'm going to teach a couple of classes as an adjunct come spring. If things don't work out with Paul, I'm going to need more money."

Pete said, "You can work things out."

"Sure, we *can*. The question is whether or not we *will*." Aaron poked at the last of his coleslaw disconsolately. "Or if Paul even *wants* to."

Chapter 34
If It Ain't Broke, Don't Fix It

After Aaron left, we tackled the kitchen together. When we were done, Pete retrieved two beers from the fridge. "Want one?"

"Sure."

We carried our bottles to the living room. I said, "After all the years of struggle. So many people making it their life's work to see same-sex marriage legalized. And for Paul to risk throwing his marriage away like this…"

"I know. It's nearly unforgivable."

"Do you think they'll work it out?"

"They have a chance. If they see Dr. Bibbins *and* if they both decide they want to."

"You think Paul doesn't want to?"

Pete made a "who knows?" gesture with his beer bottle. "I think I don't know Paul well enough to answer that."

"I hope we don't see him for a while."

"Me, too." Pete propped his feet on the ottoman. "Do you think we're getting stale in the bedroom?"

I shot him a frown. "Do *you?*"

"I asked you first."

I snorted softly. "Not this week." Thanks to rugby practice.

Pete smiled a little. "Yeah. But we stalled out some over the summer."

I nudged him with an elbow. "Not when we were alone." We'd spent a week in a hotel in Edinburgh and two weeks renting a house in Forres and had taken advantage of the isolation. Our time in Forres had almost felt like a second honeymoon.

There was a reason that romance novels featured Scottish lairds and not Santa Monica academics. The Highlands were *sexy.*

"True. But I'm not talking about frequency. I'm talking about variety. Our repertoire is so limited. I guess I'm asking if that's still okay with you."

"I don't know when it happened, but I've stopped concerning myself with that." Mostly. "Frequency is *far* more important to me than variety. As long as we keep the frequency up, I'm okay."

Pete studied his beer bottle. "But you still want to keep reading those gay romances."

"Only if you want to. I thought they might give us some ideas - although if all the ideas are anatomically impossible, maybe not."

"Those fictional guys mostly have anal."

"Yeah, but I bet they have some other tricks, too."

He chuckled. "So, just checking - we're still both committed to monogamy, right?"

"Right." I clinked my beer bottle against his. "Here's to monogamy."

He raised his bottle. "And to *rugby*."

I laughed. "I'll drink to that."

Pete turned on the TV, and my gaze fell on Guy Testaverde's novel sitting on the end table. I picked it up. "Library donation?"

"Sure."

I tossed the book onto the loveseat, and Ammo trotted over to investigate. He began to sniff the cover - which bore the image of kilos of cocaine - and I had a brainstorm. "Ammo, do you want to go back to work?"

He panted and wagged vigorously. I took that as a yes. Pete said, "Doing *what?* The cops train their own drug-detection dogs."

"I know." I pointed to the TV screen, which displayed a Weather Channel documentary on avalanches. "Search and rescue. Civilians can be handlers for that, right?"

"That's typically the case. Search and rescue, or cadaver dog?"

"Are those separate?"

"They can be. Do you intend for me to train him? 'Cause you won't have time."

"Would you be interested in that?"

He considered. "Handlers have to meet certain requirements, same as the dogs do. With my law enforcement background, I already meet most of them. I'm the one who's home with him... sure, why not?"

I said, "He's already trained as a detection dog. How hard could it be to train him on a new scent? And he sniffed out Ashley Bennett's body." Ashley Bennett was a UCLA student who was found dead in the townhouse next to ours, nearly a year ago.

Pete snorted softly. "Yeah, but it took him three days. One more day and you and I would have sniffed out Ashley's body."

"Ugh." I didn't want to remember *that* scene. "So how much training would he require?"

"I don't know. I'll ask Kevin to connect us to the LAPD K-9 trainer."

I poked him with my foot. "We've been wondering what we'd do once we move to Alamogordo. This could be one answer."

Sunday, October 1

Chapter 35
The Moment of Truth

When I woke up the next morning and checked my phone, there was a text from Kevin.

Got Mavis and Dan. Interviews start at 10:00 at our station. Wanna come?

Sure, why not?

Kristen will be there too. We'll go from the station to Neil's for the birthday party. See you at ten.

Just before 10:00, we gathered in the observation room - Hopkins, Kevin, Jon, Kristen, Pete and me. Mavis Osterhout was already in the interview room. She didn't appear to be worried but was gazing around the room with interest, a placid expression on her face. She was wearing a yellow sweater.

I wondered if there was blood on the green one.

Hopkins clucked his tongue. "Hardly looks like a criminal mastermind, does she? More like a little old lady from Dubuque."

Jon said, "Looks can be deceiving."

Kevin grunted. Hopkins said, "Okay, fellas. Let's go lower the boom on this desperado."

I said, "Show her she can't outrun the long arm of the law."

Jon snickered. Hopkins beamed at me. "You, sir, are a prince among men. And I don't mean maybe."

Kristen checked her watch. "I hate to break up this meeting of the minds, but time waits for no man. You'd better get a move on."

Kevin sighed and pulled the door open. I said to Kristen, "Even if Mavis stabbed Mercedes with one of her knitting needles, she'd have to have stood on a stool."

Jon led the way into the interview room. "Mrs. Osterhout, I'm Detective Eckhoff. This is Detective Brodie and Detective Hopkins."

Mavis smiled sweetly. "My, what handsome young men. It's a pleasure to meet you."

Kristen muttered, "Flattery will get you nowhere, lady."

Jon said, "Thank you, ma'am. Do you know why we're here?"

"Oh, yes. That nice young policewoman said that I was a person of interest in Mercedes Moran's murder, and that I could have a lawyer if I wanted one."

"Yes, ma'am. Do you want to call a lawyer?"

"Heavens, no. My daughter will give me the dickens for it, but I don't want a lawyer."

"All right." Kevin produced the waiver papers and had Mavis sign them. "You have the right to change your mind at any time."

Mavis looked surprised. "My goodness, young man. You'd think you didn't *want* to know what happened between me and Mercedes."

I chuckled. Jon said, "Trust me, Mrs. Osterhout, we do want to know what happened. When did you first meet Ms. Moran?"

"Well, it was just last Tuesday. The first day of the conference."

"Were you attending the conference?"

"Oh, no. That is, I did register for the conference but only so that I could hear the keynote speech. I came here specifically to meet Mercedes."

Jon patiently asked, "Why did you want to meet her?"

"Oh, well… I hoped that she and I could come to an arrangement."

"What sort of arrangement?"

Mavis cleared her throat. "Well, you see - she knew something that I didn't want to be made public."

"What did she know?"

Mavis folded her hands primly. "My daughter Brenda is a writer. I'm very proud of her. She always wanted to write, but she and Butch - my son-in-law - have a farm. She never had much time for anything but farming and raising my grandchildren. But once the children got older, she was able to carve out a little writing time here and there. She's written five books." Mavis smiled proudly. "They're *very* good."

"Yes, ma'am. Did Ms. Moran know something about Brenda?"

"I'm afraid so. You see, Brenda writes under a pseudonym. We live in a *tiny* town, and our church is Southern Baptist. So when Mercedes threatened to expose Brenda's real name - well. That would have been a *disaster*."

"Why?"

Mavis sighed. "Brenda doesn't just write mystery-romance novels. She writes *gay* mystery-romance novels. My youngest grandson is gay. He moved away for college, so there was no danger to *him*. But I cannot emphasize to you *enough* how conservative our town is. If people found out what Brenda did, she and Butch would be driven out of their church."

I asked Kristen and Pete, "Why the hell do they stay *in* their church?"

Pete said, "It's likely to be their primary means of social interaction, in a town like that."

Jon asked Mavis, "Does Butch know about Brenda's writing?"

"Oh, yes. Those two don't keep secrets from each other."

"Do you know how Ms. Moran learned about Brenda?"

"No. The same way she learned about all those other poor ladies, I suppose."

Kevin asked, "Did you have information to trade with Ms. Moran?"

"No." Mavis sighed. "Brenda and I searched for information on her background, but we didn't find anything. I was going to try to buy her silence."

"You were going to pay her to keep quiet about Brenda?"

"Yes."

"Did she agree?"

"No." Mavis scrunched her face up. "She said I couldn't pay her enough to keep quiet."

"Okay, we'll come back to that. How did you find out that Ms. Moran was going to expose your daughter?"

Mavis folded her hands on top of the table. "Well. You see, my grandson, Brandon, is a senior at Stanford. He knows a *lot* of people in San Francisco. He and his friends go dancing there on the weekends. Naturally, they get to know the regulars in the clubs they visit, and Brandon and his friends met Mercedes in her favorite club over a year ago. She told them she was a bestselling novelist and always bought them a round of drinks. Brandon read her blog and found out that she was telling the truth about being a novelist, but he also saw the nasty things she said about other writers."

Jon asked, "How did Brandon learn that Mercedes was going to expose his mother?"

Mavis clucked her tongue. "Mercedes told him. Of course, she had no idea who Brandon was. He'd never told her his last name, but he did encourage her to talk about her blog. Mercedes liked her liquor, and she let slip one night, just two weeks ago, that she was going to expose several writers in a speech at a public venue. Brandon wheedled the names out of her."

"Then what happened?"

"Well, Brandon called me *immediately*. He didn't want to tell his mother because he knew it would upset her. I told him to not worry, that I'd think of something to do about Mercedes."

Jon took up the questioning. "Then what happened?"

"I found out on the computer that Mercedes would be at this conference. I registered for the conference and flew here on Monday."

"Did you tell Brandon what you were planning?"

Mavis playfully shook her finger at Jon. "Now, young man. Don't you go trying to make me implicate my family. Brandon certainly did *not* know what I was going to do."

Kevin asked, "What *were* you going to do?"

"Why, bargain, of course. That was *all*."

"What happened?"

"After her speech, I followed Mercedes over to the exhibit hall. I saw the fight that she had with that other lady. When the police took her out, I followed her back to her room. She was just opening her door when I called out to her."

"What did you say?"

Mavis put her hand to her chest. "Well, you see, I did some work on the stage in my younger days. I played Ado Annie in *Oklahoma!* when I was in high school. I suspected, from what I'd read about her on the computer that Mercedes might respond well to flattery. And she did. I told her that I was a *huge* fan, that I'd read all of her books - which I did - and that I'd love to talk to her more. She invited me into her room."

Jon said, "You read *all* her books?"

"Oh, yes. They're only a dollar apiece, you know. I thought 82 dollars was well worth it." She smiled sweetly. "You know what they say. Know your enemy."

Beside me, Kristen snickered. Kevin asked, "So what happened in Ms. Moran's room?"

Mavis spread her hands. "I explained the situation to her. That I'd pay her to keep Brenda's secret."

"What did she say?"

"She *laughed*." Mavis was indignant. "She told me that she wasn't going to make any deals. We argued about it a while longer, but I was getting nowhere with her. She was so *stubborn*." She shook her head sadly.

Jon said, "What happened, Mrs. Osterhout?"

"She kicked me out of her room." Mavis sighed. "Poor Brenda. I thought that Mercedes would probably go straight to a computer and post about her, just for spite." She leaned forward, looking back and forth between Kevin and Jon intently. "I *had* to stop her."

Kevin asked softly, "How did you stop her?"

"I wasn't sure that I had, until I saw the news that evening. But I'm afraid that I'm responsible for her death."

"How so?"

"Well, as I said, Mercedes gave Brandon *all* of the names that she was going to publicize during the conference, so I had the true identities of both Angelica Ashley and Celeste Estrada. Mercedes had announced Angelica Ashley's name - Elmer Thrash, isn't that funny? - at the keynote, then that other woman - Pepper something? - stood up and said she was suing Mercedes. I remembered that and thought that *she* might be able to help me." Mavis shook her head. "I looked for her everywhere but couldn't find her. But then I was in the exhibit hall - and I spotted Dan Ross at his booth. His name was on a banner."

Kevin said, "And you recognized that he wrote as Celeste Estrada."

"Yes. I introduced myself to him and told him what I knew - that Mercedes was planning to expose both him and Brenda and that I'd tried and failed to pay her off and that I wondered if there was any pressure he could bring to bear on her."

"What did he say?"

"He got a strange look on his face. He said, 'Mrs. Osterhout, you tell your daughter not to worry. Moran isn't going to expose her, me, or anyone else. I'll handle it.' That was all he said."

"What happened then?"

"I thanked him and left. Then that night, when I saw the news report…" Mavis stopped. "I was afraid that I'd triggered Mercedes's death."

Jon asked, "Did you see Mr. Ross after that?"

"No. I didn't want to." Mavis shook her head, her eyes closed. "I didn't want to know."

Hopkins shook his head sadly. Jon said, "Mrs. Osterhout, we appreciate your cooperation. Is there anything else you'd like to say?"

Mavis sighed. "I suppose I should ask for a lawyer now."

Kevin said, "Yes, ma'am. I think that's an excellent idea."

Chapter 36
The Truth Won't Set You Free (But It May Reduce Your Sentence)

Jon escorted Mavis to a telephone. Pete flipped the intercom switch and asked Kevin, "What are you gonna charge her with?"

"I don't know. Maybe conspiracy, maybe nothing." Kevin held up his phone. "Need to call the DA."

Jon returned in a few minutes. "Mavis made her call and stopped in the ladies' room. She's in Interview 2 now with snacks."

Kevin said, "Victor Gutierrez is on his way." The assistant DA who'd recommended the Victim Impact Program to Kevin. "In the meantime, let's converse with Dan Ross. Who, by the way, has been arrested twice on domestic violence charges to which he pled no contest and was sentenced to community service." He pointed at the one-way mirror, behind which Pete, Kristen and I were arrayed. "Interview 3."

We trooped out of the room we were in - the observation booth for Interview 1 - and reconvened behind the mirror connected to Interview 3. Dan Ross was sitting in what I always thought of as the perp chair, his arms crossed. Beside him was a middle-aged man wearing golf clothes. I said, "He's lawyered up?"

Pete said, "No one in law enforcement would ever agree to be questioned without an attorney present."

Kristen asked, "D'you suppose he's ex-FBI because of the domestic violence charges?"

Pete grimaced. "Don't know if that would be sufficient to get him kicked out of the agency or not."

I said, "But it might be sufficient for Celeste Estrada fans to drop him like a rock if they found out."

Kristen said, "You'd *hope* so, anyway."

In the interview room, Dan Ross had a faint smirk on his face. I was anxious to see if Kevin could wipe the smirk off.

Hopkins, Jon and Kevin arranged themselves across from Ross. Jon opened a legal pad, and I realized that today Hopkins wasn't taking any notes.

Whatever his purpose this week, he'd concluded it.

Kevin sat across from Ross and mirrored him, arms crossed, faint smirk. "Mr. Ross. Where's the ice pick?"

Ross didn't even blink. "What ice pick?"

Pete said, "He'll be a tough nut to crack."

I said, "This will put Kevin's abilities to the test."

Kristen grinned. In the interview room, Kevin asked Ross, "Why'd you leave the FBI?"

Ross blinked at that one. Did he not think the LAPD would do their due diligence? "Because the Cheeto in Chief sacked my boss."

Ah. Earlier in the year, POTUS had fired the FBI director, creating an uproar. Kevin said, "Understandable. It didn't have anything to do with your arrest on domestic violence charges?"

Color flared on Ross's cheeks. His lawyer said, "You don't have to answer that."

Kevin said, "All righty, then. We found Mercedes Moran's neck scarf."

That did seem to throw Ross. "What are you *talking* about?"

"You had a confrontation with Ms. Moran on the morning of the day she died. Tried to strangle her with her own scarf. After Mavis Osterhout told you that Moran intended to expose you, you went back to finish the job."

"No *way*." Ross was vigorously shaking his head. "That didn't happen."

"We found the scarf. We found *skin cells* on the scarf. That means DNA. *Your* DNA."

Ross leaned forward, intent. "I. Did. Not. Strangle. Moran. I didn't see her that day until the keynote speech. And it's like you said, I didn't know that Moran knew about Celeste Estrada until Mrs. Osterhout told me."

"And you told Mrs. Osterhout not to worry about Moran or her intentions. That you'd handle it."

Jon's phone beeped with a text. He read it, grinned, and handed it to Kevin.

Kevin glanced at the screen, handed the phone back to Jon, and turned a laser gaze onto Ross. "We found the ice pick. It's *covered* with fingerprints. Do you want to bet that they're all Guy Testaverde's?"

Ross's face went blank. His attorney said, "My client has *nothing* else to say."

Chapter 38
The Icing on the Cake

We were gathered around Kevin's and Jon's desks waiting for Victor Gutierrez and a public defender for Mavis to arrive when the duty officer called Jon. "Detective Eckhoff, there's a woman here to see you. Her name's Martie Pepper."

We all looked at each other in surprise. Jon said, "Be right there," and he headed for the lobby.

He returned with Martie, who was clad in the same fashion as the first time I'd seen her - in pristinely white tennis clothing. She drew back in surprise when she saw us. "Mr. Brodie! Mr. Ferguson! Are you helping with this case, too?"

Pete said, "Hi, Ms. Pepper, it's good to see you again. We're mostly innocent bystanders on this one."

Jon said, "What's up, Ms. Pepper?"

"Please. After everything we've been through together, I wish you'd call me Martie. Anyway. I've just come from brunch with a friend who works in development with the Lifetime network. I'd originally considered producing the *Rose* trilogy with them but then decided against it." She lowered her voice and rolled her eyes. "They couldn't afford to produce it the way I wanted. *Anyway*, my friend told me that they're in discussions with another author for a romance series, but negotiations have stalled."

Jon said, "Okay... what does this have to do with Mercedes Moran?"

"The *reason* they're having issues is that the author uses a pen name and won't reveal her true identity. She, *whoever* she is, will only communicate through attorneys. Alice - my friend - said that they're starting to believe something is fishy with this author. They found out that her cover photo was a *stock* photo." Martie snorted. "One of Alice's coworkers recognized the actress in the picture."

A stock photo. Martie's narrative was starting to sound eerily familiar. Jon raised an eyebrow. "So you suspect... what, exactly?"

Martie spread her hands. "Well, here's another author trying to protect a secret identity. What if Mercedes knew about it? What if exposure would put a kibosh on the deal with Lifetime?"

Assuming that Martie was talking about Celeste Estrada/Dan Ross, I suspected that two arrests for domestic violence would put a kibosh on the deal. Kevin asked, "What's the author's name?"

"Celeste Estrada." Martie registered our reaction. "You've *heard* of her. *Is* it connected?"

Jon said, "Let's just say that the name has come up in the course of our investigation. What do you know about Celeste Estrada?"

"Well, nothing about her *personally*. I know her name because of the research I've done into Mercedes Moran. Celeste Estrada is one of her primary competitors on the e-book bestseller lists. Estrada and Moran have been writing for about the same length of time. I haven't read any of Estrada's books."

The duty officer's voice sounded through Jon's desk phone again. "ADA Gutierrez is here."

He wasn't alone; a frazzled-looking young woman - whom I assumed was Mavis's public defender - was with him. Kevin, Jon and Hopkins retreated to the conference room with the lawyers, leaving Pete, Kristen and me with Martie.

I asked, "What are your plans for filming the *Rose* trilogy?"

Martie beamed. "I just signed the contract yesterday. We're going to HBO."

Kristen said, "Wow! Congratulations!"

"Thank you. It's *so* exciting. Jessica Bledsoe is cast as Rose. This will be an enormous break for her."

Pete said, "Oh, no, will she be leaving *The Quantum Gene?* She's *terrific* in that."

"She is, isn't she? I won't do anything to jeopardize that show. We'll arrange shooting so that Jessica can do both. And you'll never guess who's adapting *Rose* for the screen."

I said, "Christopher Seagrave?"

Martie chuckled. "No, he's attached to another series that we have in the works at Gravity right now. Plus, he and Jessica are dating. Better for him not to be involved in our production. No, Trevor Nash is adapting Rose."

Trevor Nash had been attached to the *CRIMES. IN. SPACE!* fiasco. The expression on my face must have displayed my doubt that he'd be up to the task of adapting *Rose* for the screen. Martie smiled. "I know what you're thinking. But Trevor has a unique romantic sensibility that will be just right for the *Rose* story."

Pete asked, "What else do you have planned for the Gravity Channel?"

"Oh, the script that Chris is working on is for a show about a dystopian society. The 1% are living in domed cities, and the 99% are starving in polluted slums. Naturally, tensions ensue." She smiled. "Watch for it next fall."

Chapter 39
Ending Weeks of Speculation…

After another half hour, the cops and lawyers emerged. Mavis was being released and had promised to return for a trial if necessary; she accepted a ride from the public defender back to her hotel. Jill Branigan and Elias Pinter escorted Dan Ross from the building to be booked into the jail at Pacific Division; Victor Gutierrez and Ross's attorney followed them. Jon checked his watch. "Perfect timing for you to get to your party, Kev. I'll wrap up the paperwork."

"Wonderful. *Thank* you. I owe you."

I said, "What about Mercedes's scarf? Who tried to strangle her?"

Jon said, "We won't know until DNA comes back. My educated guess? Guy Testaverde."

Hopkins said, "The Tequesta Police Department will clip his wings. Mr. Testaverde won't dodge the LAPD's bullet if his dastardly deeds extend to strangling Ms. Moran. TPD will gladly toss him from their frying pan into our fire." He elbowed Kevin. "This case is one for the books, boys! Get it? Books?"

Kevin's smile looked more like a wince. "Yes, sir. Got it."

Jon said, "Would you mind answering a question for us, Lieutenant?"

Hopkins looked surprised but said, "Sure. Fire away."

"What's the real reason you were assigned to this case?"

Hopkins chuckled. "Ah, you've caught me red-handed, boys. You're right. IAG didn't send me to polish my homicide investigation skills."

Kevin asked, "Why *did* they sent you?"

Hopkins cleared his throat. "Are you familiar with the TV show *Two Days to Solve?*"

Two Days to Solve was a reality show featuring homicide detectives from big-city police departments all over the country. Each show began with a real murder and followed the cops as they solved it - or not. Jon said, "Yes, sir."

"Well, LAPD has decided that it's time to jump on that bandwagon. Naturally their inclination is to feature the best homicide team in the business. IAG sent me to screen you fellas for inclusion, and it's as plain as the nose on my face - you two are at the top of your game. I've already recommended you to the big shots. If you're interested, the gig is yours."

Kevin and Jon looked at each other. I couldn't interpret their expressions. Kevin said, "Can we have some time to discuss it?"

"Sure thing. It's not a done deal until you two give us the green light."

Jon asked, "Have you talked to our captain about it?"

"I have a meet and greet with her tomorrow morning." Hopkins nodded at Jon. "This would be a real feather in your cap in terms of moving up in the department. You'd be a shoo-in for Homicide Special with this TV show on your résumé."

Kevin said, "When we decide, should we contact you?"

"No need. Just clue in your captain. She'll spread the good word." Hopkins saluted us. "Okay, boys, it's time for me to bid you a fond farewell. It's been a pleasure."

Jon grinned. "And a good time was had by all."

I said, "All's well that ends well."

"It's sad but true. All good things must come to an end." Hopkins shook our hands. "Take care, now. It's a jungle out there."

Kevin said, "Yes, sir. It's all in a day's work."

Jon, Pete, Kristen and I burst out laughing.

When Hopkins was gone Kristen asked, "What do you think about having a TV crew follow you around?"

Kevin sighed. "It's not the most appealing proposition I've ever received. But if it'll help Jon get to D-III, it's worth it."

Jon wore a sly grin. "It might be fun."

I said, "You'd only have to try it once. If you hated it, you could give it to someone else. Max O'Brien and Susan Portman would look good on TV."

Kevin said, "Let me sleep on it. If I haven't come up with a reason not to by morning, we'll do it."

Jon beamed. "You *know* you want to."

Kevin snorted. "I know *you* want to."

Kristen said, "Come on. We have twenty minutes to get to Neil's."

Chapter 40
Happily Ever After

Neil had turned 65 on Thursday, but he and his husband Mark had postponed the family party until today. The guest list included our friend Mel Hayes, who was Neil's legal partner, and Mel's wife, Ali Fortner; Kevin and Kristen; Neil and Mel's legal secretary, Sunny, and her wife, Ellen; Jeff, Val, Colin and Gabe; Neil's sister, Anne, and her husband Wayne; Dad and Claudia, who had yet to meet the extended family; and Pete and me. In lieu of gifts, Neil had asked that we donate to the Los Angeles LGBT Center. Pete and I had sent them a sizable donation.

It was a wonderful day. We stuffed ourselves and finished with cake and ice cream. Dad and Neil told funny stories about their time together in the Marines. Dad introduced Claudia to everyone, and they were all impressed. At one point Mel sidled over to me. "Claudia and your dad seem well-suited."

"They do, don't they?" I looked across the patio, where Claudia and Neil's sister were deep in conversation.

"Your dad is different with her. He's -" Mel searched for the right word. "Lighter."

Dad was standing beside Claudia, but his ears must have been burning. He glanced over, saw us watching him and winked. I laughed. "Yeah. Val and I were talking about it earlier. He's lighthearted. He's *never* been lighthearted. He's been content, even happy at times, but in my entire lifetime he's never been lighthearted."

Mel smiled. "It sounds like that makes you happy."

"Are you kidding? It makes me delirious with delight. No one deserves a happy ending more than my dad."

"Can't argue there."

After we'd sung Happy Birthday and cut and eaten the cake, Mark poured champagne for everyone. Neil lifted his glass. "Here's to all of you, my fantastic friends and family. Thank you for making my 65 years on earth so enjoyable. I love you all."

We all said, "Hear, hear," and drank.

Neil said, "And now we have a special announcement." He gestured to Kevin and Kristen.

What?? I whispered to Mel, "Do you know anything about this?"

"*No.*"

Kevin said, "We cleared this with Neil first because we didn't want to co-opt his birthday celebration."

Neil said, "I was *delighted* to give my permission."

Kevin grinned. "Anyway, Kristen and I want to announce that we're getting married in four weeks. Saturday, October 21st."

Everyone whooped and hollered. "Congratulations!" "Way to go!" "All right!"

Pete came to my side. "Did you *know* about this?"

"No! I wonder if Dad did?"

Kristen said, "Thank you, thank you. We called Kevin's dad and my family last night to tell them, and Neil has agreed to officiate for us, like he did for Jamie and Pete. We'll get married in the back yard of my house. I've asked Val and my brother's girlfriend to be two of my attendants, and the other one will be Liz Nguyen. She just doesn't know it yet."

Everyone laughed. Kevin said, "Dad, Jeff, Jamie, will you stand up with me?"

Dad was beaming. Jeff said, "Of course."

I said, "*Hell*, yeah."

More laughter. Kevin said, "Pete, I'd like you and Jon to usher, if you would?"

Pete grinned. "You've got it."

Kristen said, "We'll have the rehearsal and dinner the evening before at the house. And, Pete and Jamie, we have a special favor to ask of you."

Pete said, "Anything."

Kristen said, "We'd like to honeymoon in New Mexico. Can we use your house?"

I laughed. "Of course you can. Sounds like you've got this all planned out."

Kevin shrugged. "We still have a few details to work out, but it's not going to be fancy. We've learned a lot from watching you and Pete and Liz and Jon get married. We're keeping it simple."

Neil said, "This calls for another toast. To Kevin and Kristen. May they have a long, long life together."

We all cheered.

On the way home, Pete said, "We need to make a trip to New Mexico. Get the house ready to be honeymooned in."

I pulled out my phone. "I'm going to text Meredith with the dates."

"Good idea."

Meredith Lagai, formerly married to Pete's brother Steve, was our full-time house-sitter in Alamogordo. After checking her calendar, she said those dates would be ideal. Steve had to make a work-related trip to Washington, DC, and Meredith would be free to house-sit for him. I texted back thanks and said, "It's all set."

Pete said, "I'm kind of surprised they're getting married."

"So am I. But it's probably a financial decision as much as anything."

He shot me a look. "That's not very romantic."

I laughed. "Oh, I'm not saying that's the only reason. They're crazy about and perfect for each other. But both of them have complicated finances. If they're married, everything goes into both names and it's much easier to manage. Not to mention it solves inheritance problems."

Pete smiled. "Claudia seemed to impress everyone."

"She did. Mel pointed out that Dad is lighter."

"Yeah, I've noticed that too. He's - different than I've ever seen him. In a good way."

I sighed happily. "Yeah. Me too."

Once we were in bed, I reached across Pete to his bedside table and picked up the romance novel we'd been reading - then laid it back down. "Real-life romance is *so* much better than fiction."

Pete smiled and took my hand, intertwining our fingers. "Not everyone gets a happily ever after."

Thinking of Aaron and Paul, no doubt. I said, "Oh, believe me, I know. But I'm thrilled that Kevin and Kristen are finally getting theirs. Not to mention - fingers crossed - my *dad*."

"I think your dad has just recently achieved the peace of mind he needed to move on. That's one positive thing that Barb did for him. She made him examine his emotions surrounding your mom and realize that he *was* partially stuck in the past."

"You're right. He had to clear out his headspace to make room for someone new."

Pete bent his left elbow, thereby bending my right elbow, and made slow circles in the air with our interlocked hands. "We're surrounded by people whose romances are going strong. Look at everyone at the party. How long have Neil and Mark been together?"

"I don't know exactly. Over thirty years, though. I guess they win the longevity prize, depending on when you start counting for Ali and Mel."

"They've been together since fourth grade!"

I laughed. "Yeah, but they didn't realize it then. Let's say they'd figured out by the time they were twelve. We were thirteen when Ali confessed to me. We're 37 now, so that's 25 years for them."

"What about Sunny and Ellen?"

"I don't know. They weren't together yet when Neil hired Sunny, and that was when I was at Berkeley. So fifteen-ish years, I'd guess."

"Jeff and Val have been together longer than Sunny and Ellen, then."

"Right. They met in 1996 in freshman biology class at Stanford. Twenty-one years for them."

"And then there's us."

I grinned and squeezed his hand. "Five years and goin' strong."

He squeezed back. "I don't want our romance to fade."

I turned my head on the pillow to look at him. "Do you think it is?"

"Not when we pay attention to it. It's easy to get distracted with the day to day crap."

I reached to the bedside table and picked up the novel again. "Maybe *that's* what these books can do for us. Serve as a reminder to assess our own romance and shore it up, if need be."

"*Yes*. Brilliant. You should order up a few more." Pete took the book from my hand and tossed it to the floor, then pulled me toward him. "But some other time."

Author Notes and Acknowledgements

Yes, it's possible for a Labrador retriever to shred an entire phone book. Mine did.

The story of how Dave Brodie met Claudia Stratton was published on my blog back in September 2017. You can find *It's A Whole New Ball Game* at https://wordpress.com/post/megperrybooks.wordpress.com/1768.

Allow me to reiterate that no character in this book is based on any *particular* real-life person. Just in case you were wondering.

Thank you to Jon Michaelsen and Matt Moore of the Gay Mystery-Thriller-Suspense Fiction Facebook group for their ongoing support.

Thanks to Frank Butterfield for the long conversations about writing gay mystery.

Thanks to Josh Lanyon for showcasing me on her blog and at her launch parties.

Thanks to Stephanie Reppas of October Design Co. for another fantastic cover.

Thanks to Dustin Weeks for the concept of AlMANzo NorWICH. Heh.

Super-duper thanks to my editor, Chris Gebhardt, who continues to make time to squeeze my books into his days between meetings with Elon Musk and writing TV pilots that are all getting optioned.

As always, thanks to my writing group: Dustin, Chris, Bryan, Michelle, Michael, Maggie, and Jenn. Our weekly meetings extend from California to Scotland now. As Lt. Hopkins would say, I never cease to be amazed at the wonders of modern technology.

Connect with me!

My blog: http://megperrybooks.wordpress.com/
My Facebook page: https://www.facebook.com/JamieBrodieMysteries/

Now, turn the page for a new short story - *Just Right: The Sequel.*

Just Right: The Sequel

Friday, October 20, 2017

I was lying in bed when I realized that the door between our bedroom and the deck was open. Pete was sound asleep. So was Ammo, which should have clued me in to the fact that I was dreaming.

In the dream, I was wearing pajamas. I slid from the bed, crossed the room and eased the screen door open. My mom was sitting in one of the Adirondack chairs, wearing jeans and a U.S. Navy t-shirt, her sneakered feet propped on the deck railing. She smiled up at me. "Hey, buddy."

"Hey, Mom." I dragged the other chair next to hers and sat. "I'm so glad to see you."

"Likewise." She leaned over and kissed me on the cheek. "This deck is terrific. The view, not so much."

I laughed. "You don't find our alley picturesque?"

"I guess it'll do for an alley." She grinned. "I understand that my Kevinbug is getting married again."

"Yep. I wish you could meet Kristen. She is *so* perfect for him."

"I wish I could, too. And Val. And Pete. I'm thrilled beyond words that you're all happy. You think Kev got it right this time?"

"Absolutely. He and Kristen are just right for each other." I gave her a sideways grin. "She's feisty. I think she might be a lot like you."

Mom laughed. "Entirely possible. I guess Jennifer and Abby weren't feisty enough, huh?"

"Jennifer definitely wasn't. I didn't know her well, but I was never sure exactly why Kev married her."

"Hm. Me either. What about Abby?"

I considered. "Abs was no pushover. She could hold her own. But Kristen is a force of *nature*. I can't say that about Abby."

"I bet your dad and Sarge like Kristen."

"Oh, Lord. The whole family is crazy about her."

It was Mom's turn to give me a sideways look. "What about this Claudia person?"

I shrugged. "We're just getting to know her. So far, though, she's made a positive impression on everyone."

Mom nodded, thoughtful. "I want Dave to be happy. More than I can tell you."

"We do, too."

We sat quietly for a minute. I said, "I wish you could talk to Kevin like this."

"I do, too. I guess it doesn't work that way. How are he and Jeff getting along these days?"

"Fine, as far as I can tell. But I don't know if either of them would admit it to me if they were fighting."

"Maybe not. You'd pick up on the tension, though."

"Yeah. And I don't sense any."

"Good." Mom shook her head. "Poor Jeff. As soon as Kevin learned to walk, he started chasing Jeff."

I chuckled. "Yeah, we've seen the home movies. Once I got big enough to play with Kevin, he stopped tormenting Jeff so much. Of course, sometimes both of us ganged up on Jeff…"

Mom poked me in the shoulder. "You shouldn't have done that."

"I know. Dad protected Jeff as much as he could. And Sarge punished Kevin and me by sticking us in separate rooms. Neither of us could stand that for long."

Mom smiled wistfully. "On Saturday, you give Kevinbug a big ol' hug from me. Okay?"

"Yes, ma'am. I sure will. Do you want to come inside for a while?"

"Nah. I think I'll stay right here. Otherwise we might wake Pete up."

I said, "Oh, Lord. You know how he is when he first wakes up."

"I sure do." She squeezed my hand. "Love you forever, buddy."

"Love you too, Mom." I stood up and smacked my forehead on something…

I woke up, in bed, pajama-less, with Pete's left forearm flung right across my head. *Ow.* I maneuvered it, slowly and gently, back to his side. He didn't even twitch.

I laid there for a while, smiling into the darkness, until I fell asleep again.

At breakfast the next morning, I said to Pete, "I dreamed about my mom last night."

"Yeah? What was she doing?"

"Sitting on our upstairs deck. She dissed the view."

He laughed. "She's right about that. She's on your mind because of the wedding, huh?"

"Yeah. That's mostly what we talked about. And she asked what I thought of Claudia."

He raised an eyebrow. "You're asking yourself what you think of Claudia."

"Apparently so."

"What *do* you think of Claudia?"

I shrugged. "What's not to like so far? But we haven't spent that much time with her."

"I thought she did well on the hike."

"Me, too." Last weekend, Dad and Claudia had joined us for a three-hour hike in Topanga Canyon. Claudia seemed to be in terrific shape physically, and she'd participated in our conversations as naturally as if she'd known us for years. "Mom said she wants Dad to be happy."

"Sure. We all do." Pete pointed his cereal spoon at me. "Kevin is getting his happily ever after. Maybe your dad's is around the corner, too."

I sighed. "I hope so."

I'd taken the day off. We were spending the entire day at Kristen's house, where the wedding rehearsal would be held this evening. While I packed swim trunks, a few toiletries and Dockers and polo shirts for the rehearsal, Pete gathered Ammo's toys and towels. We tossed our bags and the dog into the car and headed for Bel Air.

When we arrived, Kevin and Kristen were already poolside in damp swimsuits, drinking mimosas. Kevin waved a glass at me. "OJ and champagne are in the fridge. Help yourself."

Pete changed into his trunks and jumped in the pool with Ammo. I poured a mimosa for myself and refilled Kristen's glass. When I got back to the patio, Kevin had joined Pete and Ammo in the pool. I pulled a chair to Kristen's side and handed her the glass. "You ready for this?"

"What? Another mimosa?"

I laughed. "Another marriage."

"Oh, *hell*, yeah." She settled back and sipped her drink. "I can't *wait* to be a Brodie."

A thought struck me. "You're not changing your name, are you?"

"Nah. I'm too well established in my career as Ms. Beach. But I'll be a Brodie in *here*." She thumped her fist over her heart.

I grinned. "I can't wait to meet your family."

She gave me a sideways glance. "I'll be interested to see what you think of them."

"Why?"

"They're *such* hippies. I mean, they're similar to you all in some ways, and in some ways they're so different." She took a longer drink. "They haven't always approved of my choices."

"What choices? Lawrence? Daniel?"

Kristen's first husband, Daniel, had been nineteen years older than she was. Her boyfriend before Kevin, Lawrence, had been separated from his wife but not divorced. Kristen made a "pfft" sound. "No. They weren't crazy about my involvement with Lawrence, and they never warmed up to Daniel at all, but they didn't go on about either of them. They didn't think I should move to LA in the first place. 'No good will come of it,' my grandmother said. And my parents didn't openly agree, but they subtly expressed their concerns." She shook her head. "My family is all about the subtle."

"Hm. *Subtle* is not the Brodie way."

"No shit." She grinned at me. "Neither is it the Kristen Beach way. I fit into your family better than my own."

I grinned back at her. "Your grandmother was dead wrong."

Kristen smirked and raised her glass to me. "Not for the first time, either. This is terrible of me, but I enjoy proving the old bird wrong. She's so *smug*. And obnoxious about it."

"Is she your dad's mother or your mom's?"

"My dad's. She's always been *subtly* upset with him for working at the health department rather than being in private practice."

"Does your dad care?"

"Eh... it bothers him. He doesn't understand why she can't appreciate the good he's doing."

I shrugged. "She's an old lady. Sometimes that's the best answer you can come up with."

"Right." She grinned. "I can't *wait* to spring all of you on her."

After about an hour, Pete got out of the pool to shower. Dad, Claudia, Jeff, Val, Colin, Gabe, Jon and Liz were all due before noon. Pete, Val and Liz were in charge of food for this afternoon, so he needed to get ready to cook. Kristen dozed off in her chair. Ammo climbed out of the pool, shook himself vigorously and flopped down to dry in the sun.

I jumped into the pool and swam a couple dozen laps beside Kevin, then we grabbed pool noodles to support our heads while we floated, drifting around as we were gently propelled by the pool pump. I said, "I can't believe I haven't asked you this before. Does Kristen's family like you?"

He shot me a sideways glance. "Why do you ask?"

"She was telling me that her family is... subtle."

"That's true. Yeah, I think they approve. Her granny flirts with me."

"Oh, *God*."

He snickered. "I know. Kristen's mom is kind of appalled by that, too. But it's all good. Her parents are lovely people, and her brother and his partner are cool. But it's not easy to see where Kristen gets her personality. I wouldn't use the phrase *balls to the wall* to describe any of the Beaches, other than my bride-to-be."

"Sounds like maybe some of it is from her granny."

He laughed. "Maybe so."

I was about to float into the wall, so I reached out and pushed off, sending both Kevin and myself toward the center of the pool. "I dreamed about Mom last night."

Another sideways glance. "Did you?"

"Mm hm. She called you Kevinbug. Is that a real thing, or did I make that up in my dream?"

"Oh, wow." He smiled, looking at the sky. "She did, in a couple of those old home movies. You must have heard it there."

"Must have."

He drew his hand slowly through the water, watching the patterns. "Do you ever wonder how our lives would have been different?"

He didn't have to add *if Mom had lived*. I knew what he meant. "Sure. I speculate sometimes on what might have been. I don't know, though - do you think it would have made a huge difference?"

"Maybe not for you or Jeff." He waved his hand through the water again. "Not sure I'd have chosen to be a cop."

"Why?"

"I don't know... sometimes I think that if I'd been raised by someone a tad less hard-assed than Sarge, I might have decided on something like social work to begin with. Or teaching."

"Are you sorry you became a cop?"

He was emphatic. "*No*. Knowing what I know now? It's all worked out. If I wasn't a cop, I wouldn't have met Jon. I'd have never met Pete. *You'd* have never met Pete." He grinned at me. "Couldn't have that."

I laughed. "Nope. You probably wouldn't have stayed in LA after college, would you?"

"Maybe not. Jennifer didn't want to."

"And if you weren't here, I might not have come here for library school. Hell, who knows where I'd be? And with whom?" I turned a level stare on him. "But, even though you're not sorry now, there's a *but* in there somewhere."

He sighed deeply. "It's changed me in ways I don't care for."

"Hunter Mitchell." A young man who'd chosen to commit suicide-by-cop in the lounge at the Hotel Bel Air. Kevin had been the unfortunate cop.

"Yes. And, you know, people - suspects, witnesses - lie to me almost every damn *day*. About the *stupidest* things. And some of the shit I've seen, I wouldn't wish on anyone." Another sigh. "It's skewed my view of humanity, for sure."

"Yeah, but now you're doing something about it. You're nearer every day to that social work career. And you'll be *spectacular* at that."

He smiled. "You think so?"

"Not a doubt in my mind."

The smile widened into a grin. "Spectacular. That's our word of the day, huh? Tomorrow, I'm marrying the most spectacular woman in California. Maybe on the whole fuckin' *planet*."

I held up my hand for a high five. "*Damn* straight."

He smacked my hand with a grin.

Jon and Liz appeared on the pool deck about fifteen minutes later. Liz said, "You guys will be wrinkled like prunes for the rehearsal if you stay in there too much longer."

I said, "Maybe we could hold the rehearsal in the pool."

Kevin said, "Yeah, yeah. We're getting out now." He yanked the noodle from under my head, causing me to submerge for a second.

I came up spluttering, ready for battle. "Hey!" But he'd tossed the noodles onto the pool deck and was hoisting himself onto dry land.

I followed reluctantly, grabbed a towel and trailed Liz into the house. She went to the kitchen, where Pete was already holding court. I went to the shower room just off the kitchen, where Pete had left the bag with our clothes, and spent the next twenty minutes making myself presentable.

When I emerged, the Oceanside Brodies had arrived. Colin and Gabe were in the pool; Ammo had joined them. Val was emptying bags of fruit and vegetables in the kitchen; Kristen was talking to her, Liz and Pete about food.

I went outside, where Dad, Claudia and Jeff were chatting. I said, "Hey, everyone. Where's Kevin?"

Dad said, "He and Jon are finalizing the music for the reception tomorrow. You look nice."

"Thanks. These are just my work clothes."

Dad grinned. "I haven't seen you in your work clothes for a while. You even got married in cargo shorts."

I grinned back. "What can I say? I'm a casual guy." I sat beside Jeff, who was keeping one eye on the activity in the pool. "Guess you don't have to monitor the kids as closely these days."

Jeff huffed a laugh. "Only to keep them from trying to drown each other." Colin was 15 now; Gabe was 13 but nearly as big as Colin.

"How are they getting along?"

"Okay, most of the time. Gabe has a bad habit of borrowing Colin's stuff without asking, which always creates an uproar. But Gabe spends most of his free time outside, and Colin would rather be inside. So they're mostly out of each other's way."

"Is Gabe still into farming?" Gabe had always been the child who wanted to help with the garden and animals.

"More than ever. We're hoping he'll decide to take over from us eventually. Right now he says that's what he wants to do, but..."

"But he's only thirteen."

"Yeah." He sighed. "We've applied for a variance for him to attend Vista High School. They have an agriculture program with their own farm."

"Ooh, that would be cool. And it's not that far."

"Nope. Just a couple of miles beyond Mission Vista." Colin's high school.

"Do they remind you of Kevin and you as teenagers?"

He chuckled. "Sometimes. I think Kev and I were worse when we were younger, though."

I said, "I dreamed about Mom last night, and she asked how the two of you were behaving toward each other these days."

He turned to look at me in surprise. "What did you say?"

"I told her everything was copacetic, as far as I knew. It is, isn't it?"

"Of course." He turned his attention back to the pool. "That's partly thanks to Kristen. She and Val are thick as thieves. They text back and forth every day."

It was my turn to be surprised. "Seriously? I had no idea."

"Why would you? You don't spend that much time with her at work, do you?"

"No. Just at lunch. I'm with Liz far more than I am Kristen."

"Anyway, Kristen and Val being so close has drawn Kev and me closer, too." Jeff smiled, watching his boys. "It's... terrific."

I said, "It's about time."

He shot me a sideways glance. "I know. A lot of that's on me. But we're making up for lost time now."

I squeezed Jeff's forearm. "Glad to hear it."

He smiled again. "Me, too."

We sat, chatting, for a while longer. Eventually Kristen, Kevin and Jon appeared and joined the conversation. I was getting hungry and decided to act on the sensation.

I went into the kitchen, where Val was spooning deviled egg mixture into hardboiled egg whites. Pete and Liz were at the other end of the counter, doing something with spring roll wrappers. I picked a filled egg off the platter, and Val smacked the back of my hand. "Stop that. You're as bad as my kids."

"I'm hungry, and Kristen's family won't be here for another hour. Can I have another one?"

She shook her head in mock disgust and handed me the egg she'd just filled. "Don't mess up my arrangement on the plate."

"Okay." I lowered my voice. "Have you spent much time with Claudia?"

"More than you, I suppose. She and Dave have come over for dinner three times. No, four."

"What's your impression?"

"So far, she's awesome." Val replaced the egg I'd snitched from the plate. "She's funny, well-read, shares our political positions, loves dogs and wants to help on the farm. And she has her own friends that she sees frequently and has told me how much she loves her own house and garden. No negatives that I can detect."

"Good. That's how she was on our hike last weekend." I reached for a third egg, which Val handed to me. "Wouldn't it be fantastic if…?"

"If she was the one? Yes, it would." Val gingerly covered the egg tray with aluminum foil and slid it into the fridge, then began to fill a second tray. "Jeff and I have discussed this - Kristen's the real deal, obviously, and it seems like, just *maybe*, if Claudia turns out to be the real deal…"

I said, "Our family will be complete."

"Exactly." Val smiled at me. "I know no one will ever replace your mom, but… Your dad is different with Claudia than I've ever seen him. He's - I don't know - *lighter* somehow."

"Mel said *exactly* the same thing. That's a perfect description." I held out my hand for another egg. "I believe my mom would like Claudia."

"From what I know of your mom, I think so, too." Val handed me another egg. "That is your *last* egg, mister."

"Okay, okay." I grinned at her, slid off the stool and went to the other end of the counter.

Pete handed me a small bowl and a whisk. "Stir that. Gently."

"Okay." I peered at the reddish substance in the bowl. "What is it?"

Liz said, "Sweet and sour sauce. I don't want it to separate."

I stirred, gently. "Liz, I think Jon needs to lay a charm offensive on Kristen's grandmother when she gets here."

Liz chuckled. "He does enjoy the old ladies. Why?"

"From what Kristen said, she's the most likely of the Beach family to be - um - irascible? Although Kevin did say that she flirted with him. But we don't want her doing that today, right? Or bothering Kristen in any way? So maybe Jon can keep her occupied."

Pete, who was mincing carrots, laughed. "Remember that night in Oakland, when he dragged me into escorting that flock of librarians? He was like the Pied Piper. They'd have followed him anywhere."

Liz said, "You made a superb team. You should help him out with Kristen's granny."

He paused, knife in mid-air. "Oh, no. He doesn't need *my* help to deal with one little old lady."

I said, "Kristen got her take-no-prisoners attitude from *somewhere*, and it wasn't her parents. I think her granny might be a handful."

Pete frowned and attacked the carrots with renewed energy. "You could do it just as well."

"No, I can't. I'm a groomsman. I need to stay available."

"For what?"

I spread my hands. "For emergencies. It's a *wedding*. Shit happens. You're just an usher. You don't have to be responsible for anything."

Liz was laughing. "Pete, you're not gonna win this one. Besides, if she starts flirting with Jon, he may need a distraction to extricate himself."

Pete scraped the carrots into a large bowl and attacked a head of cabbage, grumbling. "Okay, fine. But Jamie, if I appear to be in distress, you'd better consider that an *emergency*."

I grinned. "I promise."

An hour later, the food was made, Colin and Gabe were dry and dressed and it was time for Kristen's family to arrive. We watched from the front porch as a battered blue Subaru wagon eased through the gate and putted up the rise in the driveway. Beside me, Pete muttered, "This is like a scene from Downton Abbey."

I snickered. The Subaru stopped in front of the porch steps, where my entire family - including Jon and Liz - was lined up in what did resemble an Edwardian receiving line. The doors opened and five people emerged.

Kristen's family.

My immediate impression was that her parents and brother should have auditioned for roles as elves in the Lord of the Rings movies. They were tall, like Kristen, but more willowy. Her parents could pass for siblings at a distance. Both had long silver hair, braided, hanging halfway down their backs. Her brother had lighter hair than Kristen's, shaggy but nowhere near as long as his parents'.

Kristen's brother's girlfriend was a young black woman, also tall and willowy, with chin-length dreadlocks. Kristen had told us that she was Jamaican.

Kristen's granny was tall for an elderly lady, but not as tall as the rest of the Beaches. Her gaze swept all of us and landed at the end of the line, on me.

I grinned at her. She seemed to be perplexed by that, but smiled at me anyway.

Kristen's dad went straight to mine. "Dave, I'm so pleased to finally meet you. I'm Tom Beach."

Dad shook Tom's hand vigorously. "Same here, Tom. We've heard great things about you."

Tom smiled, and I saw where Kristen got her wide, happy smile. "Likewise." He turned to his wife, who'd been hugging Kristen and Kevin. "Janie?"

She switched her attention to Dad. "Hi, Dave. I'm Jane Devereux."

Tom said, "This is my mother, Helen Beach; Kristen's brother, Parker; and his girlfriend, Zara Reid."

A flurry of introductions later, we all helped the Beach clan haul their luggage into the house and up the stairs to their respective bedrooms. Liz, Pete and Val set out the feast of cold finger foods they'd created. We filled plates and gathered around the pool.

Pete and Jon, as we'd discussed, sat with Kristen's granny and poured on the charm. I ended up in a corner with Liz and Claudia. We watched as Kristen skillfully wove a web of conversation around

Kevin, Dad, Jeff and Val and her own family. I said, "Claudia? You okay with this?"

Claudia was concentrating on her food. "Hm? Oh. Yes." She waved a cheese-laden cracker in the direction of Dad. "Dave and I discussed it. I'm still getting acquainted with all of *you*. I didn't think I should horn in on the parental getting-to-know-you chat. Dave didn't exactly agree, but I insisted."

I said, "They're not what I expected."

Liz asked, "How so?"

"I'm not sure. Kristen had described them as down to earth people. But they're so…" I frowned, searching for the right word.

Claudia said, "Ethereal."

"*Yes*. That's it. Kristen is many wonderful things, but *ethereal* she ain't."

Liz said, "Kristen has reinvented herself considerably since coming to Los Angeles. Maybe she used to have some ethereality that got burned off in the smog."

Claudia laughed. I said, "Maybe her family hasn't figured out how to shift their previous image of her with the grownup version."

Claudia said, "I may be reading this wrong, but - I believe her family is somewhat in *awe* of her."

We watched for a minute. Liz said, "Hm. I think you're right."

I said, "I agree. But why would they be? Her dad's a doctor and her entire family is accomplished." Kristen's mother ran a CSA and food co-op in Yakima; her brother spoke several languages and worked as an interpreter in the King County court system in Seattle, and Zara was pursuing a doctorate in biochemistry at UW.

Claudia said, "Money."

Liz and I both looked at her in surprise. I said, "You think the Beaches are impressed by money?"

"I think they're impressed that *Kristen* has money. She's risen from their comfortable middle-class existence into the rarefied air of millionaires." She laughed. "Not that any of you *act* like millionaires - which is part of the awesomeness."

Liz said, "I bet the Beaches had no idea what to expect from the Brodies. How much time has Kevin spent with them over the past two years?"

I said, "A few days here and there. Not much."

Claudia said, "They might be a bit overwhelmed. The Brodies *en masse* are formidable."

I said, "*You* haven't been overwhelmed."

She laughed. "I can hold my own."

"And *that* is why my dad likes you. One of the reasons, anyway."

Liz said, "You're a pretty astute observer of the human condition, Claudia."

"I spent nearly twenty years in pharmaceutical sales. Being able to read people is an asset."

I grinned. "As it is for reference librarians. Right, Liz?"

She snorted a laugh. "*Oh*, yes. The bartenders of academia, that's us."

Claudia got tickled at that. In another few seconds, the three of us were hooting with laughter. Kristen glanced over at us, a bemused smile on her face, then crooked her finger. *Come here*.

Claudia wiped her eyes. "You two are being summoned."

Liz and I gathered ourselves to the extent possible. I said, "You should come with us."

"No." Claudia grinned. "I'm going to join Pete and Jon. They might need a break."

Liz and I ended up perched on the edges of lawn chairs. I was forced to gingerly balance to avoid sending Jeff - my seating companion - flying into the pool, which limited my ability to produce scintillating conversation.

Kristen was saying, "Jamie and Liz are librarians, too. We've worked together for years."

Kristen's mother - Jane - smiled at me ethereally. "You introduced Kristen to Kevin, didn't you, Jamie?"

"Yes, ma'am." I scooted back, inadvertently pinching Jeff's leg against the chair. He grunted and tried to shove me off with a knee to the ass. I planted my feet and held my ground.

Kristen's dad - Tom - said, "I understand you were a Rhodes Scholar."

"Yes - *unh* - sir." I grunted as I pushed back against Jeff, who was now actively attempting to dislodge me, the bastard. I reached behind myself and punched what I hoped was his knee, not taking my attention from the senior Beaches.

Jeff hissed, "*Ow*," and smacked at my arm.

Dad, who I thought had been in deep conversation with Kristen's brother, said - without even glancing our way, thanks to years of practice - "You two cut it out."

Jane and Tom smiled, subtly. Kevin and Val smirked, openly. I decided to yield and stood up. "Does anyone need a refill on anything?"

Jeff scrambled to his feet as well. "I'll help."

We collected a few glasses and plates on a tray and headed into the kitchen. As we passed Pete, Jon, Claudia and Kristen's granny, Pete glanced up at me and rolled his eyes.

I wondered what that was about, but it didn't seem that emergency relief was needed.

Jeff and I walked into the kitchen and stopped, horrified by the stacks of dirty bowls and utensils left behind by the cooks. I said, "Shit. This is a *mess*, and there are caterers coming later. Let's clean this up."

"Okay." Jeff refilled glasses for Parker and Zara. "Be right back."

"You'd *better*."

"I *will*." He disappeared out the back door.

I began clearing dirty dishes from the sink so I could fill it with hot water. Jeff returned as promised, with Jon and Kristen's grandmother on his heels.

Jon was saying, "Don't worry about a *thing*, Mrs. Beach. I'll make sure you don't miss the rehearsal."

"You are just the *sweetest* young man." Mrs. Beach patted Jon's arm. "You could teach my grandson a few things…"

Jeff and I looked at each other in dismay. Jon continued upstairs with Mrs. Beach, then thumped back down the steps and into the kitchen. "*Damn*. That woman is something *else*."

I said, "Grab a dish towel. How so?"

"She's taking a nap before the rehearsal." Jon lowered his voice anyway. "She's not exactly a cheerleader for either of her grandchildren, but Kristen's brother gets the worst of it. 'He can't do *anything* right.' Direct quote."

Jeff, who was washing dishes, plunged his hands into the soapy water I'd run. "Jeez. What's her problem?"

Jon dried the first bowl and handed it to me. "Guess."

I guessed, as I put the bowl away. "Granny Beach is a little bit racist?"

"Bingo." Jon took another bowl from Jeff. "I mentioned something about my Asian wife, just to see what she'd say. She's like, 'Oh, the Japanese are lovely people. My husband and I had a Japanese gardener for years. Such a pleasant man.'"

I said, "*Japanese?*"

Jon scowled. "She just *assumed*."

Jeff snorted in disgust. "Good thing you kept her away from everyone else, then."

"Yeah." Jon handed me the dry bowl. "I don't wanna have to spend any more time with her, though."

Pete came in as Jon was speaking. "Where'd she go?"

"She's taking a nap."

"Good." Pete shook his head. "What a piece of work. No wonder Kristen wanted to move a thousand miles away from her."

I said, "Your charm offensive didn't work?"

"Oh, it worked." Pete perched on a barstool. "She thinks Jon and I are wonderful. The feeling isn't mutual."

Jon said, "I usually *like* little old ladies."

Pete made a "pfft" sound. "I think that one is beyond redemption."

I said, "You should have told her you were Native American. Just to see what she'd say."

"Pretty sure I know what she'd say." Pete leaned over the counter and snagged a spring roll. "But then Claudia rescued us."

Jeff asked, "She handled Granny?"

Jon said, "Yup. Got her talking about her bridge club, smooth as silk. I think your dad has a keeper, guys."

Jeff and I glanced at each other. He said, "We hope so."

An hour later, the kitchen was clean and ready for the caterers to arrive. We had about a half-hour before the rehearsal's scheduled start time. I was tying a garbage bag closed when my phone buzzed with a text.

It was from Scott Deering, whose cello quartet was providing the wedding music. *We're here. Can someone open the gate?*

On it. I hit the button to open the gate and stepped onto the porch to see a familiar black Mercedes SUV come through, followed by two other cars. Scott parked in the paved area to the right, and he and an older woman got out of his car. The other two cars were occupied by men, probably in their forties. All four arrivals removed cello cases from the vehicles. Scott led them to the steps and grinned up at me. "Hey."

"Hey yourself. Need any help?"

"Nope." He stopped and indicated his companions. "Jamie Brodie, this is Verna Ziegler, Marshall Clarke, and Antoine Baptiste."

I shook hands with the cellists. "Pleased to meet you. I'm the brother of the groom."

Verna, Marshall and Antoine all greeted me. Scott asked, "Where are we supposed to set up?"

"Out back. Come on through the house."

I led the way through the foyer and kitchen to the patio where Kristen spotted us and hurried over, her arms open for a hug. "Scott! It's so good to see you."

"You, too." Scott hugged back then looked around the space. "Which side do you want us on?"

"Over here." Kristen showed them to the corner of the paved area. "I thought you'd rather not be on the grass."

"You're right. Thanks."

Kevin and Dad appeared, and Scott repeated the introductions. Kevin said, "Thank you for being here."

Verna said, "It's our pleasure."

I thought, *I bet, for what you're probably being paid.* But I knew that any quartet of Scott's would be worth every penny. I drifted to Scott's side as he and the others unpacked. "How's everything?"

"Fine." Scott gave me a knowing look. "Ethan says hello."

"Ah. You may return the sentiment. Are you keeping him under control?"

He laughed. "Yes. He needs to be bossed sometimes."

"Well, you're up to *that* challenge."

"Uh huh."

Kristen brought her parents over to introduce to the musicians, and there were several moments of subtle politeness. I noticed that Parker and Zara were alone on the other side of the patio and made my way to them. Zara smiled as I approached. "Hi. Jamie, right?"

"Right. How are y'all doing?"

"Oh, we're fine. The food was *outstanding*."

"I'll pass on the compliment. Liz, Val and Pete are all fantastic cooks."

Parker said, "Pete is your husband, right? He's the one who cornered my grandmother."

"Right. Kevin had sort of warned us."

Zara shook her head, her dreads bouncing. "She hates me. I don't care."

Parker said, "She hates both of us. It pisses me off, but all we can do is stay away from her."

I said, "You all live in Seattle, right? If I remember my geography correctly, there's a mountain range between you and Yakima."

Zara grinned. "Yep. Mt. Rainier and all of her friends. I *adore* mountains."

I chatted for a while longer with Parker and Zara on happier topics, mostly about academia. About fifteen minutes later, Neil and Mark arrived. Neil Anderson, a Marine buddy of my dad's who'd known us since we were born, was performing the ceremony. He'd done the same for Pete and me two years before. His husband, Mark Sivak, waved to me - and I was struck with an idea.

I excused myself from Parker and Zara and made my way to Mark. Neil was already taking charge, talking to Kevin and Kristen and gesturing to different points on the patio. I said, "Hey, Mark, how's it hangin'?"

He grinned. "All is well. I assume the elvish people are Kristen's family?"

I laughed. "You noticed that too, huh? Listen, I have a mission for you, should you choose to accept it." I told him everything I knew about Kristen's grandmother. "She needs a keeper for the evening. Would you mind? You're the only one here who doesn't have another assignment."

He clapped me on the shoulder. "No worries. Leave her to me."

"*Wonderful*. Thanks, Mark. I owe you."

He waved that off. "I'll consider it a gift to Kevin and Kristen. Point me in the direction of this harridan."

Jon had escorted Mrs. Beach back to the patio. They were near the door; she was hanging onto his arm and yammering about something. I steered Mark in that direction. "Mrs. Beach? This is Mark. Jon has to usher, so Mark's going to spend the evening with you."

Mrs. Beach brightened at the prospect of yet more male attention. "Oh, thank you. How lovely of you to think of me."

Mark kissed the back of her hand. "Mrs. Beach, it's an honor. Where would you like to sit while everyone else arranges themselves?"

Jon and I left them and headed toward the knot of people that comprised the rest of the wedding party. Jon said, "Brilliant. Did you tell him everything?"

"Yep. He's up to the challenge."

Jon shook his head. "Better him than me."

Scott and the quartet began to play, running through the first few pages of several pieces. When they'd paused, Neil stuck his fingers in his mouth and whistled. "All right, everyone, let's gather. The quartet will begin playing thirty minutes before the ceremony, as Pete and Jon are seating the guests. Once it's 3:00, I'll take my place with Kevin, Dave, Jeff and Jamie, then the quartet will begin the processional. Pete and Jon will seat Kristen's grandmother and mother, then the bridesmaids will proceed. Have you ladies decided in which order you'll enter?"

Liz said, "Zara first, then me, then Val."

Kristen said, "Take your time. I want everyone to hear as much of the processional as possible."

Scott and his fellow cellists laughed. I whispered to Jeff, "What's *that* about?"

He shook his head. "No idea."

Neil said, "Once the bridesmaids are in place, Kristen and her dad will process. Tom will be seated, Kristen will take her place beside Kevin, and we'll say the vows. Shall we run through that much?"

Pete, Jon, Kristen, Val, Liz, Zara, Kristen's mom and granny disappeared into the house. Scott and the quartet began another piece. Granny reappeared on Jon's arm, walking slowly. It seemed that she was taking every moment possible to bask in the attention of everyone. Once she was halfway down the aisle, Pete took Jane's arm and escorted her to the front-row seat beside her son, separated by one seat from her mother-in-law. Pete and Jon retreated to the back, and Neil signaled Scott. Scott nodded to the others, then laid his bow across his lap and began playing his cello like a string bass. I didn't recognize the intro, until another of the cellists - Antoine, as I remembered - began strumming the cello strings as if they were guitar strings.

Pachelbel's Canon - except in a way I'd never heard it. Jazzed up and dance-worthy. I found myself fighting to stand still. Verna joined the fun, playing quick staccato notes, and Marshall turned his cello into a drum, beating out the rhythm.

It was awesome.

Zara danced her way down the aisle first. Liz waited until she had reached the front then used the music to perform an energetic hula as she processed. I knew Val wasn't much of a dancer, so I had no idea what she might do.

I shouldn't have worried. Once Liz was in place, Val moved as if the song being played was Boot Scootin' Boogie, adapting those moves to the music. Beside me, Jeff was laughing his head off.

Val slide-stepped into her place, grinning at Jeff. Then we turned for the main event.

Kristen was holding a spatula as a bouquet substitute. She must have forgotten flowers and grabbed it at the last minute. Kevin started laughing when he spotted it. Kristen and her dad didn't dance as energetically as the others - there wasn't room in the aisle - but they took their time, shimmying and stepping. Tom twirled Kristen a couple of times, then twirled her again as a method of depositing her into her spot beside Kevin.

We were all laughing by that point. Scott and the quartet wrapped up the music with a sudden stop, and everyone on the patio applauded wildly - except Kristen's granny, who applauded politely.

The cellists stood and took a bow. Neil called out to Scott, "What *was* that?"

"Pachelbel as interpreted by The Piano Guys." Scott grinned. "Check 'em out on YouTube."

"I will." Neil turned back to us. "Okay. At this point I will say a few words about marriage, then we'll repeat the vows, then we'll exchange rings. Dave, Val, you're responsible for that."

Dad and Val nodded their assent. Neil said, "Then I'll pronounce that Kevin and Kristen are married and we'll recess. Kevin and Kristen first. Then Dave and Val, Jamie and Liz, and Jeff and Zara. We'll practice that now. Scott?"

Scott lifted his bow, signaled the other cellists and they began playing "Happy Together." Kristen and Kevin grinned at each other and danced back down the aisle.

Dad and Val proceeded a bit more sedately. I grabbed Liz's hand and twirled her at the head of the aisle, then we followed Dad and Val. I asked Liz, "Had you heard this music before?"

"Yeah. I helped pick it out. We had to choose a couple of months before the engagement, even, to give Scott and his quartet time to learn the music."

"Good thing they're some of the best cellists in the world, then."

"Yup. Wouldn't have worked otherwise."

Once we were all at the back of the patio, Kristen said, "That's it, everyone. Kevin and I alone will comprise the receiving line and greet the guests as they come into the house to eat. The rest of you get to serve yourselves first."

Kevin added, "Consider it a perk of standing up with us."

Kristen said, "We'll eat outside as much as possible. Once everyone is eating, we'll cut the cake then have the first dance."

Pete asked, "Should Jon and I rearrange the folding chairs in a more informal pattern?"

"*Yes*. Excellent idea."

Mark said, "I'll help."

Kristen clapped. "Perfect. Obviously I've allowed a *few* things to slip my mind…" She waved the spatula in the air. Everyone laughed.

The caterers had arrived, and I was delighted to discover that the food was from Eugenio's, my favorite Italian restaurant, where - if my memory served - Kevin and Kristen had spent their first date. I was also pleased to see that Neil and Mark were on either side of Kristen's granny, being solicitous.

Which meant Pete was free, and I was finally able to sit down with him for dinner. We commandeered the patio chairs where Liz,

Claudia and I had been sitting earlier in the day. Pete dropped into his seat and said, "*Whew.*"

"No kidding. Somewhat more involved than our wedding rehearsal, huh?"

"Somewhat." Pete sliced into his eggplant parmesan. "I don't think I've ever asked any of you - what was Jeff and Val's wedding like?"

"Super-informal. They got married in a field of wildflowers on Val's parents' farm. Jeff wore jeans with sneakers and a button-down shirt, and Val wore a simple white dress and wellies."

Pete laughed. "Sounds about right. Who were her bridesmaids?"

"Two of her college friends and her oldest brother's wife. He was the only one of the boys that was married then." Val was the second of five children, the other four all male.

"Was Kevin's first wedding in a church?"

"Yeah, in Julian." Kevin's first wife, Jennifer Graham, was a native of Julian, a tiny town in the mountains of San Diego County. "It wasn't very religious, though. Kev and Jennifer had asked the minister to take it easy with the God stuff. He did. Jennifer only chose to get married in the church because that's what her family preferred."

"So both of Kevin's weddings will be more formal than ours or Jeff's."

"Yeah. Who'd have predicted that?"

Pete grinned. "I've been replaying our own wedding in my head on and off all day."

"Me, too." Although probably not as often as Pete had. But I wouldn't tell him that. "Where are you and Jon gonna sit tomorrow?"

"Huh. I don't know. Why?"

"Because I want to be able to lock eyes with you when Kev and Kristen are saying their vows."

"Awwww." Pete beamed. "We'll set aside two chairs for ourselves on the front row on Kevin's side. I'll be able to see you; Jon will be able to see Liz."

I maneuvered my left leg to wrap my ankle around Pete's right one and beamed back at him. "Perfect."

As everyone finished eating, the energy of the group died down. Kristen's granny declared her fatigue, and Mark escorted her inside. Parker and Zara visibly relaxed once she was gone.

Dad and Claudia were in a corner chatting with Kristen's parents. Kevin and Kristen were eating with Jeff, Val, Parker and Zara. Jon and Liz were hanging out with Scott and the other cellists. Colin and Gabe were lurking behind their parents, occasionally disobeying my orders to not feed Ammo from their plates. When Mark returned from the house, he and Neil sat with Dad and Claudia.

I finished my lasagna and leaned back in my seat with a deep sigh. Pete glanced at me with a grin. "You sound content."

"You betcha. Although part of me wants to collect plates and glasses."

He chuckled. "Shocking."

"I know. I'm predictable."

"Only when it comes to cleaning." Pete gestured at Claudia and Dad. "Claudia seems perfectly comfortable at your dad's side... and vice versa."

"Mm hm." I watched them together for a few moments. "Val described Dad as *lighter*."

"Yeah. I can…" Pete interrupted himself with a jaw-cracking yawn.

I laughed. "It is getting late. Maybe we should go, then everyone else will?"

"Excellent idea." He reached for my plate. "I'll take these inside, and you round up your nephews."

"Will do." Colin and Gabe were spending the night with us to provide their parents with a mini-break from parental duties. Dad and Claudia were staying in Kristen's fourth guest bedroom; Kevin and Kristen were spending the night at their condo, with Jeff and Val as guests.

It took a while for Colin and Gabe to collect their belongings and say goodnight to their parents, but by 10:00 we had both boys and the dog in the car and were headed home. Gabe said, "Uncle Jamie? It's a special occasion, so can we stay up late?"

I said, "No, sir. It's a special occasion, so you have to go to bed on time."

"But…"

I held up a finger. "No arguing."

Gabe acquiesced reluctantly. "Okaaaay."

Colin said, "I have homework this weekend."

"You're not doing it tonight. You've got all day Sunday."

"But…"

I held up a finger and gave him The Look.

He grumbled but gave in. "Okaaaay."

Pete was trying not to laugh.

At home, I prepared the sofa bed in our office for Colin while both boys brushed teeth in the guest bath and Pete collected sheets and pillows for Gabe's night on the sofa. Jeff had warned me that it was best not to make them sleep in the same bed.

I heard Gabe thump down the stairs. Colin came into the office and dug through his backpack, extracting pajamas. I said, "Where's your iPad?"

He sighed heavily, retrieved a tablet from his backpack and handed it to me. "Here."

"Thank you." Val had instructed me to confiscate electronics from the boys so they'd go to sleep. "You can read a book for a while if you want. Did you bring one?"

"Yeah." Colin showed me a fat biography of Robert Oppenheimer.

"Whoa. Is that for school?"

He snorted. "No. Uncle Steve recommended this one."

"Ah." Pete's brother Steve was a physicist working on propulsion systems for the Air Force. "Okay. Anything else you need?"

"Nope." Colin crawled between the sheets. "G'night."

"Night, buddy." I closed the door and went downstairs where Gabe was attempting negotiations with Pete. "Gabe. You are *going to bed*. Where's your iPad?"

He pouted but dug it out of his backpack. "Here."

"Thank you. Did you bring a video game?"

"No. Mom wouldn't let me."

"Good." I retrieved the TV remote and added it to my stack of contraband, which produced a deeper pout in Gabe. "Do you have a book to read?"

"Yeah." He rooted around in the backpack again and showed me. *The Omnivore's Dilemma* by Michael Pollan. "Can Ammo sleep down here with me?"

"Sure." I turned to the dog, who was nosing around Gabe's backpack, and pointed to his supplementary bed at the foot of the sofa. "Ammo? Bed."

Ammo complied, circling three times then flopping down with a doggie sigh. I said, "Good boy. All set, Gabe?"

"Yes, sir." Gabe smiled up at me angelically. "Night, Uncle Jamie and Uncle Pete."

Pete said, "Night. See you in the morning."

I said, "And not before."

Gabe grinned. "Okaaaaay."

Pete and I double-checked the locks and retreated to our own room. Pete dropped onto the side of the bed and began tugging off his socks. "Whew. I'm glad you rescued me. Gabe was wearing me *down*."

"What did he want?"

"His iPad. 'Just for school stuff, Uncle Pete, honest.' Batting those baby blues at me."

I laughed. "Gabe's a charmer. He's more like his Collins cousins." Val's brothers' kids.

Pete pulled his polo shirt over his head and threw it at me. "I bet you were a charmer in your day."

I tossed his shirt into the laundry basket. "I could have been, if I'd had anyone to charm. Sarge wasn't having any of *that*."

"I guess not." Pete hung his pants up - my training was finally paying off - and went into the bathroom. "I guess we'll be throwing weddings for Stephanie and Samantha one of these days."

Pete's nieces were in college; Samantha had just started at UCLA four weeks ago. "No time soon, I hope."

"Probably not. They're both pretty career-driven at this stage."

I joined Pete in the bathroom to brush my teeth. "Weddings are a blast for close families like ours, huh? Not so much for the Beaches, though. Poor Parker and Zara, forced to spend hours confined in the same space as the old lady."

He grunted as he joined me at the sink. "Yeah. Some families get along better when they're separated by hundreds of miles."

"It's too bad. But I'm glad, in one way. It means Kristen is eager to join *our* family. Both Jennifer and Abby always wanted Kev to spend more time with *their* families. Kristen will be one of *us*."

Pete mumbled around his toothbrush. "She already is."

Saturday, October 21

I dreamed that we were at Jon and Liz's wedding. Pete and I were sitting in the back, on either side of Kristen's grandmother. The Buddhist priest was talking about the Six Perfections. Mrs. Beach was squirming.

I leaned to her and whispered, "Are you okay, Mrs. Beach?"

"Oh, yes. But this is dragging out a bit, don't you think?" She sighed deeply. "The Japanese are lovely people, but *really...*"

Pete made pancakes for breakfast, then he took the boys and Ammo to the dog park while I cleaned house. By the time they returned and everyone was showered and dressed, it was noon. Time to go.

We picked up the pizzas that Kevin had pre-ordered at 800 Degrees and drove to Bel Air, where we found Liz and Claudia fussing with seating arrangements. Jon was at a laptop, checking the reception music; Kristen was consulting with Dad and Val about... something. Kevin greeted us at the door and helped carry the pizzas in. I said, "Where are the Beaches?"

"Gone to the Mt. Wilson Observatory." Kevin began sorting through varieties of pizza. "I'm glad to get 'em out of the house for a while."

"Granny went, too?"

"Yup." He completed a stack of margherita pizzas. "They'll be back soon."

Pete and I wandered around for several minutes in search of a way to help but were shooed away by everyone. We gave up, filled plates with pizza and headed for the pool deck. I was halfway through my plate when Kristen's family returned. I heard their voices ethereally floating to my ears for a few minutes, then nothing.

Maybe they'd gone upstairs to get dressed.

Dad joined us shortly thereafter, three slices of pizza on his plate. I said, "How was your night?"

"Fine. Claudia and I stayed up pretty late sitting out here, but we didn't hear a peep from the Beaches." He shook his head. "They're pleasant enough, but they're... not exactly what I was expecting."

I had to agree. Pete said, "Families often have a - not a black sheep, necessarily - let's say a dark horse. One member who causes people to wonder how that person came from that family. Kristen is the Beaches' dark horse."

Dad nodded. "Kristen has finally found the family she belongs to. It's us."

I held up a pizza crust. "Here's to *our* family."

Pete and Dad grinned and tapped my crust with their own.

At 2:15, Scott and the other cellists arrived. I didn't have a chance to speak to him; they took their places, tuned, and began to play.

Liz's cousin, Mickie, the restaurateur, arrived with a handful of her workforce to prepare food for the reception. I didn't see a cake but assumed Kristen had it stashed somewhere.

Drew Jemison - whose mom had been killed with ours while out with Belinda Marcus, who'd played with us as toddlers and had become a friend as an adult and who was now working for Ali on her xeriscaping crew - stuck his head out the back door and spotted me. "Hey, I'm the official photographer. Anything I need to know?"

"I guess not. All the action is happening on the pool deck. I didn't know you were a photographer."

He shrugged. "It's a hobby, but it brings in some extra money. And I've started taking before and after pictures of our landscaping jobs for Ali's website."

"Cool!" I waved at the quartet. "I guess you can start with them."

Drew unslung a bag from his shoulder, produced a camera with a long lens and began taking photos. Pete had been helping in the kitchen but collared me as I hovered near the door to the patio listening to the quartet. "Come on. We'd better get dressed."

"Oh, okay. Whose room are we using?"

"Dave and Claudia's."

I trotted up the stairs behind Pete. From behind the door to Kristen and Kevin's bedroom, I could hear the chatter of Kristen, Liz and Val. I assumed Zara was in there, too.

Pete and I entered the guest bedroom, and suddenly it was *crowded*. Kevin was draped over an armchair by the window; Dad was retrieving his suit from the closet; Jeff was overseeing Colin and Gabe as they dressed.

Jon was buttoning his cuffs, frowning into a full-length mirror. "How do I look?"

I said, "Suave and debonair. As always."

He snorted. "Right. Pete, we'd better get downstairs. Guests will be arriving any minute."

Pete donned his suit and tie somewhat hurriedly. He and Jon enlisted Gabe and Colin's assistance with ushering duties and herded them out of the room.

Which left the original Brodies. Dad, Jeff, Kevin and me.

I dressed in my best suit, dove gray with the pink shirt and pink-and-gray striped tie that I always wore with that suit. Jeff and Dad had new suits, both dark gray. Jeff's shirt was blue, his tie navy; Dad's shirt was white, his tie red. Once we were dressed, we got out of Kevin's way.

I asked, "How does it feel this time, compared to marrying Jennifer?"

Kevin grinned into the mirror as he looped his tie - aqua and gray striped. "A thousand times more right."

Jeff said, "You think this is it, huh?"

"I *know* it is." Kevin wiggled the knot nearly closed on his tie and turned to face us. "*You* know it is. Kristen was *made* for our family."

Dad chuckled. "I can't argue with that."

Jeff agreed. "The way she and Val hit it off? On the way home from Jamie's wedding, Val said to me, 'Kristen's a keeper.' She knew as soon as they met."

I said, "I didn't think either of you would get married again."

"Neither did we." Kevin buttoned his cuffs - white shirt - and slid the jacket of his black suit over his shoulders. "And it's not like we had big discussions about it. We just kind of said, 'Let's get married.' We actually tried to think of reasons not to and we couldn't."

Dad said, "That's a pretty strong indicator."

"Yep." Kevin settled the jacket on his shoulders and looked in the mirror again. "The family fuckup finally gets it right, huh?"

Jeff and I looked at each other in dismay. Dad grew very still. "What did you say?"

The expression on Kevin's face said, *Shit, did I say that out loud?* He said, "Uhhhh…"

I said, "I think we should see if everything's ready." I took Jeff's elbow, ready to steer him toward the door.

Dad said, "You two stay put."

We stayed.

"Sit." Dad pointed to the bed.

We sat.

Dad crossed his arms and turned his attention to Kevin, but his expression was softer than it had been with us. "Explain yourself."

Wasn't Kev talking about his lack of marital success? He shrugged, palms pointed at the ceiling. "We-eeelll… There's Dr. and Dr. Happily Married Geniuses there and then there's me."

"Has either of these so-called *geniuses* said *anything* to you to promote that line of thinking?"

I felt Jeff tense beside me. Kevin said, "No, sir. Not for years."

I figured I knew when the last time was - the fight we'd all had after we'd visited the office of Gordon Smith, the attorney who handled our inheritance from Randall Barkley. Over two years ago. Jeff had insulted us both that day.

Dad said, "Remind me what your grade point average is, in your social work program."

"Four point oh."

"Uh huh. And remind me what that Latin phrase is on your college diploma."

"Summa cum laude."

"Uh huh. Do you seriously believe that one entirely justified divorce and one other entirely justified breakup constitutes fucking up?"

"Well…"

"How many breakups has Jamie had?"

I opened my mouth to interject, but Jeff elbowed me. Hard.

Kevin shot me an apologetic look. "I'd have to count."

Fair enough. So would I.

Dad said, "So would I." He took a step closer to Kevin and said softly, "Tell me. Have I ever said *anything* to you that made you believe that you were a fuckup?"

Kevin's denial was immediate and vehement. "No, *sir!*"

Dad asked, "So why the hell do you have this idea?"

Kevin shrugged again. "Well… It's just the way it is. The firstborn and the baby are special. I'm the one who was always making trouble."

He'd had plenty of help from me in making trouble. I opened my mouth, but Dad shot me a look and I closed it again.

"Have I ever had to bail you out of jail? Or send you to rehab?"

"No, sir."

Dad studied Kevin for a moment then said, "Do you believe for some reason that you were less *wanted* than those two?"

Kevin didn't squirm very often, but he was squirming now. "Um... not really."

"You'd *better* not. Believe me, you were *every bit* as carefully planned as those two were. We couldn't *wait* to meet you." Dad's face relaxed into a smile. "When the nurse handed Jeff to me, about ten minutes after he was born, he kept right on crying. When I first held Jamie, he immediately dropped off to sleep. Do you know what you did?"

"No, sir."

"You opened your eyes and gazed right at me, like you were studying me. I slid my finger into one of your fists, and you latched on as if I'd thrown you a lifeline. We stayed like that for at least five minutes. I knew right then that I was in for the ride of my life." Dad jerked his head in our direction. "Neither of those two looked at me for at least a week."

I wished Dad would stop referring to Jeff and me as "those two." Kevin said, "I didn't know that."

"Jeff might not agree, but you never made any trouble that was serious. You were the one that Sarge and I never had to worry about. Jeff was a hypersensitive introvert. Jamie was asthmatic. Both of them required some extra attention because of those things. Maybe that meant we shorted you in the attention department some, and if so, that's on us. But it wasn't because you were less deserving; it was because you were less needy. You came to us *just right*."

Kevin swallowed, hard. My own eyes were beginning to mist up. Dad said, "So deep six the fuckup shit." He moved toward Kevin until they were nearly nose to nose.

I had to smile - Dad and his Maxi-Me. Dad put his hand on Kevin's cheek. "You are my just right boy. Don't you *ever* forget that. Understood?"

Kevin whispered, "Yes, sir."

Dad pulled Kevin into a long hug. Tears were streaming down Kevin's cheeks. I wiped my own eyes just as Neil stuck his head in the door. "It's about that time."

Dad and Jeff headed down the stairs, but I pulled Kevin back for a second. I had a promise to fulfill.

He frowned a little. "What?"

I pulled him into a hug. "This is from Mom."

We hugged for a good ten or fifteen seconds, then I pulled back. Kevin was wiping his eyes again. "Well, shit."

I laughed and darted back into the bedroom for tissues. "Here."

"Thanks." He dried his face and blew his nose, then grinned at me. "Let's go get me married."

I grinned back. "All righty then."

We lined up behind Neil - Kevin, Dad, Jeff and me - and proceeded out the French doors to the patio, around the pool to the podium and platform. Pete and Jon were seating the last of the guests; Colin and Gabe were already seated in the front row. I scanned the crowd. On Kristen's side, I spotted our library friends: Dr. Loomis, whose husband was too ill to attend, sitting beside Isabella Gutierrez and her husband, Assistant District Attorney Victor Gutierrez; Justin and Lance, sitting with Andy Narahashi and Jessie Gaither; Connie Bright and her husband; Lesley Cabot, our interlibrary loan librarian, and her husband; Frank Villareal and his wife; Katrina Johnson and her oldest daughter; and Dolores Lopes and her husband, who were sitting with Lola Mack. I knew Kristen had also invited Ruth Brown, but she'd had a family event of her own that conflicted.

On Kevin's side were Ali and Mel; Ali's parents, Charlie and Bev Fortner; Ali's sister, Lauren, and her husband Dustin; Kevin and Jon's boss, Tim Garcia, and his wife; Jill Branigan and her boyfriend, who I believed was a firefighter; Elias Pinter and his wife; Max O'Brien and his husband, who I remembered was an ER doctor; and several other cops whose faces I recognized but whose names escaped me.

Drew was behind the seated guests, his face obscured by his camera, moving as he snapped photos.

Neil gave Pete and Jon the high sign, and they nodded, disappearing into the other set of French doors. Scott's quartet finished the piece they were playing - or at least came to a stopping point - and began the first processional. Jon came back out first, with Kristen's grandmother on his arm; Pete followed with Kristen's mother. They got the ladies settled, then took their own seats on the front row on Kevin's side.

The quartet stopped for a moment, then began playing the jazzed-up version of Pachelbel's Canon. Zara, Liz and Val came down the aisle next, dancing even more joyfully than they had at the rehearsal. They were wearing varying shades of turquoise and aqua - Zara had woven matching beads into her dreads - and they all looked fantastic. I snickered when I saw that Val was wearing cowboy boots. Liz stuck her tongue out at me as she took her place; I wrinkled my nose at her.

All of the guests were grinning widely. A few were even dancing in their seats.

Finally, Kristen appeared on her dad's arm. She was wearing a simple pale aqua dress, sleeveless and knee-length, flared just a bit from the waist down. She was stunning. I could see Kevin's face from where I was standing; he was beaming from ear to ear.

Tom twirled Kristen into place, and Scott and the quartet stopped playing. Neil gazed around the gathering until he had everyone's attention, then said, "Dear friends and family, we are gathered here to witness…"

Kev and Kristen, unlike Pete and me, had chosen the standard vows rather than writing their own. When Neil came to the "for better or worse, richer or poorer…" section, I turned my eyes to Pete, whose gaze turned to mine at exactly the same time. We exchanged surreptitious grins. When Kevin said, "I do," I mouthed to Pete, "Me, too."

He responded silently, "Me, too, too."

Kristen repeated her vows, and Neil pronounced them husband and wife. I wondered if they'd kiss, but I should have known… Kevin and Kristen grinned at each other, lifted their right hands and firmly bumped fists.

The crowd burst into laughter and applause. Scott nodded to the quartet, and they launched into "Happy Together" as Kevin and Kristen danced back down the aisle.

Scott's quartet was done for the day but were invited to stay for the reception if they wished, at least to eat. The three cellists that we didn't know filled plates with food and began to mingle. Scott sidled up to me. "Okay with you if I stay for a while? Ethan's grading papers all day and won't surface until this evening."

"Of course. Stay as long as you like."

We - the families - lined up for photos while the guests ate, then filled our own plates. While we ate, Kevin and Kristen cut the cake; Gabe and Colin distributed slices to everyone. When most people's plates were clear, Jon took his place at the computer as DJ. Kevin and Kristen went to the center of the room, and Kristen cued Jon.

Kevin and Kristen's first dance was Christina Perri's "A Thousand Years." It was perfect. Afterward, we all applauded. Kevin and Kristen grinned at each other, then turned to the crowd. Kristen said, "All right, all of you. Come on."

Almost all of my former boyfriends - Ethan, Nick, Eric and Scott - had been enthusiastic dancers. I didn't remember exactly how I'd learned to dance, but the ability had been a handy device. During high school dances, I'd always stay on the dance floor, hence avoiding awkward small talk and unwanted female attention.

My usual partner in high school was Mel. She had studied ballet, jazz and tap since toddlerhood and was a fantastic dancer. At our high school prom, she and I had won the award for Best Dancer Couple.

Ali wasn't a dancer, unless it was a country line dance. Val's skills were limited to the same arena. Jeff, to my knowledge, had never danced, even at his own wedding. Pete wasn't a dancer either. He could shuffle from foot to foot in rhythm, but that was the extent of his ability to boogie. He said he'd never attended dances in his youth so had no reason to learn.

Kevin, like me, had used dancing as a way to avoid unwanted entanglements with random girls at high school events. He'd even entered a dance-a-thon once with a girl he was dating at the time, and they'd sambaed and tangoed their way to second place.

I didn't know Kristen's history with dance.

Jon pushed a button, and the first riff of Walk the Moon's "Shut Up and Dance" filled the room. I grabbed Mel by the hand, and we never looked back. "Uptown Funk." Justin Timberlake's "Can't Stop the Feeling." Pharrell's "Happy." Maroon 5's "Sugar." "Good Vibrations," which apparently convinced cellists Verna and Antoine to join the fun. "The Twist," which drew Dad and Claudia, the Gutierrezes, the Garcias, and the Pinters to the floor. "Best Day of My Life" by American Authors. The B-52's "Love Shack," which inspired a few more cops to join the fray. Coats and ties were tossed aside and sleeves were rolled up; the women were kicking off their shoes.

Scott and Liz were dancing together. Justin and Lance, Andy and Jessie, and Frank and his wife were dancing. Jill Branigan and her boyfriend, and Max O'Brien and his husband were dancing. Parker and Zara were dancing. I laughed when I saw that Gabe was dancing with Katrina Johnson's daughter, who I thought was only eight years old but who already had some great moves.

After about 45 minutes, the crowd had become amorphous, sort of a mosh mob centered on Kevin and Kristen. I saw Mark offer to relieve Jon, who accepted, then cut in on Scott and whirled Liz away.

I was dripping with sweat and needed a drink. I handed Mel over to Scott and worked my way to the coolers lined against the house, from which I snagged two bottles of Carlsberg and headed for our table. Jeff, Val and Ali were in deep conversation. I dropped into the seat beside Pete and handed him one of the bottles. He accepted it gratefully and grinned at me. "Tired?"

"No, just dehydrated." I clinked my bottle against his. "Here's to Kevin and Kristen."

He clinked back. "Indeed."

I drained about a third of my beer and spotted Drew, circling the dancers, snapping photos. "Drew seems to be enjoying himself."

"Yeah. I hope the pictures are good."

"I'm sure they will be. Where's Granny Beach?"

"Neil escorted her into the house a while ago. He may be trapped."

I snickered. "Neil can hold his own."

"Yup." Pete slung his arm across the back of my chair. "I'm glad to see your Dad and Claudia gettin' their boogie on."

"Right? Claudia's a terrific dancer."

"Your dad's not bad, either."

I nodded, watching Dad and Claudia. "I didn't know that about him."

"How would you? He hadn't met anyone he wanted to dance with until now."

I sighed. "I sure hope this works."

"Me, too."

I stayed beside Pete for about a half hour as we watched and commented on the various dancing styles on display. Gradually, the tempo of the music slowed, starting with Al Green's "Let's Stay Together." When Lonestar's "Amazed" began, Val dragged Jeff to his feet. I saw Scott and the other cellists head for the coolers and Mel beckoned to Ali.

I nudged Pete. "Wanna dance?"

"Nah…"

But the next song convinced him. "God Only Knows." He stood up and took my hand. "Let's dance."

We joined the mass of bodies on the pool deck. I took both of Pete's hands, held them against my chest and sang to him as we swayed. "But long as there are stars above you…"

He sang back, tears in his eyes. "God only knows what I'd be without you."

CPSIA information can be obtained
at www.ICGtesting.com
Printed in the USA
BVHW03s0045050618
518234BV00008B/140/P